Kimi's Fear

The sequel to Kimi's Secret

JOHN HUDSPITH

Copyright © 2012 by John Hudspith

The moral rights of the author have been asserted.

All rights reserved. No part of this publication may be reproduced, distributed, or transmitted in any form or by any means, including photocopying, recording, or other electronic or mechanical methods, without the prior written permission of the publisher, except in the case of brief quotations embodied in critical reviews and certain other non-commercial uses permitted by copyright law. For permission requests, write to the publisher, addressed "Attention: Permissions Coordinator," at the email address below.

Cover design and formatting: JD Smith

Printed in the United Kingdom by FeedARead.com Publishing.

All enquiries to info@johnhudspith.co.uk

First printing, 2012

ISBN

www.kimissecret.co.uk
www.johnhudspith.co.uk

For Lola and Nathan.
May your crows be happy,
your fish divine,
and your monsters grinning.

`*Understand before you bleat, man. You're killing the world, you know.*` - **Monster's Chronicles**

`*The thing under my bed waiting to grab my ankle isn't real. I know that, and I also know that if I'm careful to keep my foot under the covers it will never be able to grab my ankle.*`
- Stephen King

`*You have to know the magic before you can see the magic.*` - **Monster's Chronicles**

`*Fiction is the truth inside the lie, and the truth of this fiction is simple enough: the magic exists.*` - **Stephen King**

Contents

1	Déjà Vu	13
2	Beware the Walleyed	21
3	No Worries	29
4	EAT ME	39
5	Area 51	51
6	A Hero's Welcome	63
7	The Thieving Crow	79
8	The Remorseful Crow	95
9	DRINK ME	109
10	There's No Place Like Home	119
11	The Briefing	133
12	Phenate Thrawn	147
13	`One death today`	161
14	Devine Intervention	179
15	Humility Served	207

Previously in *Kimi's Secret...*

With a deformed hand and a fondness for Marmite and animal skulls, Kimi Nichols was as normal as any other girl - until visited by a talking crow who prophesied death shortly before a colossal lightning bolt exploded right above the golf-course where her parents were playing.

Confronted by Bentley - her childhood imaginary friend - Kimi was whisked to the paranormal dimension of Heart where adepts rule, monkeys enforce the law, aliens are greylians, roasted dodo is always the dish of the day... a place where she will be safe.

But safe from what? With help from Stella - Kimi's assigned mentor - they uncovered the terrible truth; her parents were dead, killed by the lightning. Kimi learned her parents were balancers, and that she was too (albeit a premature). Following clues left by her father, Kimi uncovered a hidden adept and the culmination of her father's life's work: the formula for successful time-travel.

Kimi was given a secret never to be revealed, mastered her mojo, and travelled back in time to save her parents. Enlisting the aid of a greylian General to complete the jump through time and across dimensions, Kimi discovered that the lightning bolt was greylian-made, her parents were murdered, and the murderer was her pilot who wanted Kimi's brain – the Secret.

But mercy came in the form of the doppelganger paradox; the greylian General was consumed by his own stupidity as he and his double began to disintegrate. Kimi fired up her mojo and finished him off by blowing a hole in his gut.

Reunited with her parents, Kimi returned to Heart to meld with her old self and set time straight again. She succeeded but sent ripples through Heart which brought eruptions and quakes and a whole lot of damage. All balancers were evacuated to Earth space while rebuilding took place.

And now, a year has passed…

Nowhere…

They cross dimensions with elegant ease, two crows, wings tucked, bodies spiralling in corkscrew fashion; the sucking winds of mind and space propelling them to their destination.

Bursting into Earth space in a whirlwind of feathers, hurtling through a grove of orange trees and to wherever their beaks will lead them, soaring above the trees, wings thrashing madly, waiting for a turn, a lead, a sign.

And there is an oak tree, its crown like a spread of open claws. They allow the pull, alight on the uppermost twigs, hop down into the thicker branches, find a good perch.

Destination reached.

By the turquoise pool outside a white stone building, their target throbs like a beacon; two girls with yellow hair, basking in the sun. The sender had warned this would be a tricky one. They should observe before making an entrance. But there is a problem. The target is protected within a huge cage of mesh. No way in.

One of the crows lets out a disgruntled caw…

1
Déjà Vu

The safe-house: Acorn Sundew Villa, Kissimmee, Florida.

"Did you hear that?" Kimi got up from the lounger.
 Stella lifted her sunglasses. "What?"
 "Stella, that was a crow."
 "What was a crow?"
 "It just cawed – from over by the oak tree."
 "Didn't hear nothing. Sorry."
 "How could you not hear that?"
 "I was dozing… dreaming of the massive party we're going to have when we get back."
 "It was definitely a crow."
 "Ach, we've seen the odd crow round here before. What's to worry about?"
 "It didn't sound… right." Kimi went to the mesh screen which surrounded the pool area and protected it from bugs. She looked out at the oak tree.
 "Could've been a grackle," Stella offered.
 Grackles looked like crows but nicer. Nicer in that their

feathers shone and glimmered. They always reminded Kimi of the famoose back on Heart. "It wasn't a grackle. Grackles are cute. It was a crow. From over there."

Stella came to Kimi's side, and together they stared at the old oak, the biggest tree on the Sundew complex.

"Can't see nothing," Stella said.

Kimi continued staring at the tree, aware her breathing had got heavy.

"You all right, sister?"

"I - I'm sorry. It's just…just a feeling, you know?" She did not let on that Little Hand was tingling - tingling for the first time in almost a year - a year in which they'd been holed up in this boring old safe-house; a villa among fifty others, all luxurious but each more like a prison to its hidden guests. Since the evacuation from Heart when Kimi's cross-dimensional jump through time brought the green mount sliding down on Middling, balancers and their tulpas had been hidden in safe-houses all over Earth. But hidden much longer than was planned. The disappearance of a greylian General had brought death threats and stirring talks of war. There was a bounty on Kimi's head – or to be more accurate: her brain. The time difference between the two worlds meant that almost sixty years had passed on Heart since the day that time turned inside out - and Kimi was nervous about returning. Getting the nod to eventually go back must mean greylian relations had got a lot better, but still, there was always that threat, that constantly looking over your shoulder half-expecting to see the bulbous head and oily black eyes of a greylian looming over you – or worse – another talking crow. Kimi would be the last to return to Heart, and with that moment only two days away, she was absolutely terrified.

"You going to stare at that tree all day?"

"Huh?" Kimi spun round. Dad was standing at the sliding doors. He had changed into his business suit.

"We're going soon. Remember?"

"Déjà Vu," Kimi said. She took Stella's hand and dragged her inside.

Mum, also now in her business suit, was sitting at the kitchen island with a green Rabbit's Foot napkin tucked in her blouse, eating pancakes that Rehd had served up.

To see Rehd, the great monkey, chief of fuzz, serving up pancakes for almost a year, was something that tickled his chimpanzee wife, Ruthie. She tweaked his stubby nose and kissed him. Rehd blushed as he always did, though it is hard to tell when a monkey blushes. He was wearing blue shorts and a tee-shirt with `Kong Rocks` on it. Kimi wondered if he'd be taking his newfound fashion back to Heart.

"Is everything okay, lovely?" Mum said.

"Yeah… I'm good." Kimi joined the crew at the island. She smeared Marmite on a pancake, rolled it up, nibbled at it.

"Just you look a bit worried."

"Going to miss her momma," Ruthie said, grinning. Ruthie had taken to dying the fur around her neck and shoulders a deep red. She also wore lipstick and false lashes. "Ain't you, sweetie?" She snacked on bliss gum.

Rehd brought a jug of pommy juice and began filling glasses. Kimi smiled at him.

"It's only for a couple of days," Stella said. "I'll so miss your hair."

"What?"

"Your hair. When you dye it back to black. Ach, we're like proper sisters when we're both blonde."

Dad tapped the remote. The doors to the pool area slid shut. "Okay, listen up people. You all know the drill, but we need to go over it one more time before we leave." From his notes he ran through a list of reminders: *Never leave the complex unless in an emergency. Balancers Cready, Fitstart, and Stubbs are always on standby if you need them. Never use mojo outside, unless in an emergency. Keep a low profile at all times. Keep the screen door locked. Blah, blah, blah, blah, blah.*

"Oh, and most importantly of all?" He waited.

Ruthie raised a furry paw. Her nails gleamed with purple polish. "The walleyed," she said in a sinister voice. "Beware the walleyed!"

"Absolutely correct!" Dad said. "I'm sorry for going on, but I can't emphasise it enough. If you see a walleyed, a human – man, woman *or* child – whose eyes seem too far apart, and maybe their forehead's a bit bigger than is normal, then you can bet your life you are seeing a greylian-human hybrid. And those things will be looking for *you*!" He gazed around, at Kimi, at Stella, at Rehd and Ruthie. "See a walleyed, get questioned by a walleyed, you give your false name and get out of there. Understood?"

"He's so clever, your papa," Ruthie said. She ran a purple claw down Dad's cheek. He smiled and flushed a little.

"Right," Kimi said. "Too clever, sometimes."

"What's that supposed to mean?" Dad swallowed the last of his pancake.

Kimi shrugged.

"You do look a bit off colour, you know," Mum said. She removed her napkin bib and wiped her mouth. "But I'm sure it's nerves, you know - like going back to school after the summer holidays. Everything'll be fine. You'll see."

"Sorry," Kimi said. "Guess I am just nervous about going back. And you and Dad will have been there for four months before I get there, what with the time diff. I guess I'm missing Bentley, too."

"Aye, and Big Sue," Stella said.

"Of course, and Big Sue," Kimi said. Bentley and Big Sue had returned to Heart a week ago to help with rebuilding and to prepare the Rabbit's Foot for reopening. Being parted from one's tulpa was not a good feeling.

"But we'll only really be gone for two days," Mum said. "Now, chin up. Good times ahead."

"I like it here," Rehd said, climbing onto a stool. "I'm going to miss the place." He took Ruthie's hand, kissed it. "What about you, my little chunky monkey?"

"How can you like it here when you're not even allowed outside?" Kimi said before Ruthie had chance to reply.

"He likes the commercials on TV, and the good food and the hot weather," Ruthie said. "And we can go out to the pool and bask. We love basking, darling, don't we-" She scratched Rehd's chin. He closed his eyes and sighed.

"Right then, Val," Dad said to Mum. "We best be off. Anyone got any questions? Any worries?"

No one had. Or at least no one voiced any.

They left the island and went upstairs to the first landing closet where four suitcases waited at the door. This was the designated twirly room; the only place in the villa that wasn't protected by Velostat. Velostat lined the villa's walls and ceilings and prevented penetration from greylian abduction beams. The problem was that it also interfered with twirly transmission, so the small closet was deemed appropriate and was always kept locked. There were hugs all around and Mum and Dad stepped inside with their cases. The room was bare, shuttered from the outside, lit by a single light bulb sat in the ceiling. Dad waved, Mum blew a kiss. Stella pulled the door shut on their smiling faces. A swish of wind from inside was followed by a cold breeze coming from under the door, a quickening roar – and then silence.

Stella opened the door. Gone.

"So, what is it, Balancer Nichols?" Rehd said, back downstairs at the island.

Kimi looked at him.

"I've lived with you for almost a year, served you a zillion pancakes, I know when your head's aching – and sometimes your heart. Something's bothering you."

There was an awkward silence. Stella broke it: "She thought she heard a crow."

"I did hear it," Kimi said.

"We've heard crows before," Rehd said. "It's nothing."

"This – this was different. The noise, the caw, it wasn't – natural – as if-"

"Where did you hear it?"

"Outside at the pool."

"When?"

"Just before we had pancakes."

Rehd pressed the remote and the doors to the pool slid open. Kimi followed him outside.

"I can hear grackles," Rehd said. "No crows."

Kimi stared at the oak tree.

"You've nothing to be afraid of anyway. It could never get inside the screen," Rehd said. "So let's relax inside, have dodo pizza, and curl up with *The Little Mermaid*. It's at least a week since we watched it."

"I guess." Kimi placed Little Hand on Rehd's head and ruffled his thick black hair. "I was afraid of you when we first met, when you pulled up on your shiny squad and did your strutting thing. You were a cheeky monkey."

Ruthie scampered through the doors and leapt onto the lounger by Rehd's side. "He still is," she said, squeezing his bottom. Ruthie was wearing a pink sequined tutu over denim dungarees.

Rehd sighed. "I *will* miss this place."

Stella joined them and they all stared through the mesh. The big oak sat still and lazy in the sun. There was a breeze that rippled its golden leaves.

Goosebumps ran up Kimi's arms.

"We should go inside," Ruthie said. She took Rehd by the hand and led him indoors.

Stella turned to follow but Kimi stopped her. "Something's wrong," she whispered.

"Ach, you've just got the heebie-jeebies."

"No," Kimi said. "There's something wrong with *me*."

Stella looked worried. "Like what?"

"Shush – keep it down."

"What do you mean there's something wrong with you? Since when? And why didn't you tell your folks?"

"I was worried it might delay me from going back. But the thing is -"

"What?"

"I can't show you here. Let's go to our room."

***

2
Beware the Walleyed

Once inside their ensuite bathroom, Kimi locked the door, took a jar of makeup remover from the cabinet, unscrewed the lid, and stroked a cotton ball across the gel. "Promise me you won't tell a soul."

Stella leant against the sink. "Okay."

Kimi leaned in to the mirror and rubbed at the sides of her nose with the cotton ball. When she was done she faced Stella. "There, what do you make of that?"

Stella came up close. "You've got two black spots, one either side of your nose."

"As if I didn't know."

"They're just freckles, or moles, or something. No biggie." Stella shrugged.

"That's not all." Kimi took another cotton ball, stroked it in the gel, and began wiping her left elbow.

"You've got concealer on your elbow?"

Now Kimi wiped the right elbow. She held both up to Stella. At the point of each elbow, right on the bone, another small black spot, the skin around it a little cracked and swollen.

Stella shrugged again. "It's just dry skin or something.

Too much sun, you know."

Kimi shook her head. She slipped out of her trainers and pulled her socks off. She held one heel up to Stella, and then showed her the other. Stella gasped.

The skin around each heel was greyed and dry, each ankle blackened. Dark featherlike shadows fanned out from the heel upwards.

"Now I know why you stopped wearing your flip-flops," Stella said.

"Yes, now you know."

"This reminds me of something," Stella said. "That time with Blavatsky's Greylian when she did the Cortell and your hand went black and icky and turned into a -"

"Claw - yes - that's exactly what I was thinking. It's the crow in me trying to get out."

"You should have told your folks. This could be serious. You could be ill. Dying even. You can't keep this to yourself, Kimi. Do you feel okay?"

Kimi sat on the toilet and pulled her socks on. "I've been feeling weird for a few days - since I first noticed the marks. But today I feel worst of all. I feel as if I'm being watched."

"Ach, it's probably because your folks were leaving today. Course you're going to be a bit jittery. Your birthday's coming up next week, you're going back to Heart in two days. It's just nerves. That's all."

"That's just it. I don't want anything to spoil *this* birthday."

Stella came and hugged Kimi. "We won't let it. We'll have a big do in the Foot."

Kimi let out a long sigh.

Stella unlocked the door. "C'mon we're going for donuts. My treat."

"There's something else," Kimi said. She held up Little Hand, her left hand, smaller than the right, crisscrossed with grooves in the flesh. "I got tingles today. Tingles for the first time in a year."

"That could be nerves as well," Stella said. "You know, like your body is on high alert, making your senses sharper, just in case."

"In case?"

"Well – look, you need to stop worrying. Let's go for donuts."

"You're forgetting something."

"What?"

"There's a crow out there."

Stella closed her eyes. It looked like she was counting to ten. When she opened them they twinkled over a forced smile. "If there's a crow, I promise you I will violate safe-house protocol and whack said crow with a volley of stunners. That okay?"

Kimi thought for a moment. "No, it's not. Promise that if there's a crow you'll let me deal with it."

"Whatever, just let's get those donuts." Stella opened the door and left.

Kimi looked at Little Hand, flexed it as far as it would go. No tingling. She followed Stella.

Rehd and Ruthie were sprawled over the comfy sofas watching *The Little Mermaid* on the plasma screen. Stella told Rehd where they were going and what for, like she always did. Rehd asked for chocolate donuts to be added to the order, and that was that.

"He doesn't seem too bothered about us going out," Kimi said as they stepped through the sliding doors.

"Course he's not bothered. You've got the heebie-jeebies and today is just another boring day in our Florida jail."

They went around the pool to the screen door. "Hang on," Kimi said. She scanned the area outside the mesh. One or two people walking. Two or three grackles searching the lawns for worms. That's all. Little Hand remained silent.

"Good to go?"

Kimi nodded. They both put on sunglasses and Stella opened the screen door. They set off walking, hurrying past the oak tree. Kimi could feel eyes on her back as they left it behind. It gave her the shudders. Balancer Alia Stubbs, a slender woman with honey-blonde hair which fell past her shoulders and who always dressed in black, was tending her garden. Alia was unusual in that she had *two* tulpas: Caitlin, a sleek and shiny brown cat with white hoops on her tail, and Emily, a bright white owl with enormous blue eyes and little pointed brown ears. Apparently, Stubbs almost drowned as a kid, and Cat and Em turned up in a boat to save her.

Caitlin was rolling around on the lawn with a ball of string. This made Kimi smile. Cat the cat was tiny, a kitten really, and the ball of string was bigger than her. She stopped playing and gave them a wink. Kimi winked back. Emily, a tall owl with great poise, was perching on the porch; her head swivelled, saucer eyes following Kimi and Stella as they passed. "Twit," Emily said. Stubbs winked and twitched her nose. Kimi smiled in return then linked arms with Stella and they hurried along the pathways between villas.

The row of shops situated on the south side of the complex was as far as they were allowed to go. A whole year in Florida and they hadn't even done a theme park or a water park, something Kimi vowed to put right one day, but then again, as Dad had pointed out, once you've flown in a greylian craft and hurtled through time and space no theme park ride would ever be as exhilarating.

"I need more concealer 'n' stuff," Kimi said. "You get the donuts while I go to Mac's"

"Okey dokey." They crossed the narrow street. Stella disappeared into JJ's Donut Heaven while Kimi went up the road to Mac's Pharmacy. There were a dozen or more people, walking, talking. Kimi scanned for walleyed. She'd never come across a real one, only saw pictures that Rehd kept in a file. Women, men, and kids, eyes almost on the sides of their heads, foreheads a little larger than normal. None of the people here looked suspect. She slipped into Mac's, quickly filled a basket with six tubs of moisturiser, six jars of makeup remover, two dozen tubes of concealer, three bags of cotton balls, and a bottle of bubblegum pink nail varnish.

Mac marked it up to Dad's account, packed everything into two paper bags, apart from the nail varnish which Kimi pocketed, then Mac asked her if she was setting up her own business.

"Going away for a while. Stocking up," she told him, and left the store quickly, where she came across a young boy of around four. He wore baggy shorts and a black and white stripe tee-shirt. He was concentrating on the mouth of the Monster machine by the wall outside. Put a dollar in and the monster spits out a plastic ball with a toy and candy inside. Kimi guessed the boy had no dollar. She scanned the people, looking for the boy's mum or dad, and considered sticking a dollar in for him, when a big white truck pulled up outside the steakhouse on the corner. Little Hand tingled and Kimi froze. *The Baby Prawn Co.* logo appeared in bright orange letters on the front of the truck along with a smiling plastic prawn stuck to the grille. The driver, in orange dungarees, got out, pulled up a side shutter and removed a box - then the truck started to roll forward.

Kimi spun round. The little boy's arm was right inside the machine's delivery slot. He was starting to whine.

"Georgie?" A woman's voice. "Where are you, Georgie?"

"Hey!" the driver yelled as the truck rolled away from him. "Hey! Hey! Heyyyyyy!"

He must have forgotten to put the handbrake on. It was only a slight incline, but the truck was big, heavy, and picking up speed.

"Georgie! Georgie!"

"Get out of there!" the driver screamed.

The truck bore down in silence, five or six tons of rolling metal.

The familiar warm glow appeared behind Kimi's brow. A heartbeat later and mojo was flooding down her arms. Her right arm tensed, she spun, her shopping bags falling to the floor, and she smashed a forearm into the Monster machine. It shattered. Plastic balls bounced everywhere. Little Georgie fell free. Kimi scooped him up and flung him into the arms of his arriving mother whose mouth seemed frozen in a perpetual scream. Then the truck, its chrome grille and the grinning plastic prawn was almost upon her, inches from crushing her against the wall. She raised her hands and they met the front of the truck. She nudged backwards a little, face to face with the grinning prawn, her back touching the wall. The truck had stopped. The driver arrived, sweating an expression of puzzlement. If anyone looked close enough they might see that Kimi's hands weren't touching the truck at all. There was a thin barrier of mojo separating her from the truck's weight and it was taking all her concentration to hold it. "Get it off me! Now!" Kimi ordered.

The driver jumped into the cab, started the engine and reversed a couple of metres. He got back out. "How did you-!?"

"Oh Georgie, you saved my baby," the woman was crying and so was Georgie.

Stella was there with a donut box, tugging Kimi away. They stumbled through the mess of broken jars, plastic balls and the jagged remains of the Monster machine – and Kimi came face to face with a big round camera lens. Behind it, a man in a blue Hawaiian shirt, a baseball cap on backwards, and sunglasses. Kimi's own sunglasses were hanging half on and half off. The man pressed the button and the camera flashed.

"Helluva trick you did there, little lady." He snapped off two more pictures. "What's your name?"

"Huh – Huh - Henrietta Blanche," Kimi said as Stella dragged her away. The man took off his sunglasses and watched them go. Kimi couldn't be certain, but his eyes looked way too far apart.

"What *were* you thinking," Stella said as they entered the pathways of the Sundew complex.

"I – I didn't have a choice," Kimi panted.

"That was bloody stupid, Kimi."

They hurried on, passing villa after villa until the oak tree came into view. Both Stella and Kimi skidded to a stop.

The caws were loud and repeated over and over.

Not one, but two black shapes emerged from the branches, silhouettes of wings flung wide, claws outstretched, coming straight at them.

***

3
No Worries

Kimi came to at the same time as Stella. They were on the comfy sofas. *The Little Mermaid* had been paused. Balancer Stubbs was standing over them, Caitlin the cat on one shoulder, Emily the owl on the other. Dangling from Stubbs's outstretched finger were a pair of crows trussed up with string, beaks tied shut. Both crows were snoring. Rehd and Ruthie were standing with arms folded. They looked rather cross.

Kimi's head was fuzzy, but it was all coming back to her. Just as she'd been about to blast the arriving crows, Balancer Stubbs had leapt onto the path between them, freezing her and Stella with an icy flash from her eyes, while behind her, Emily had sprung from her perch, knocked the descending crows from the air, and Caitlin had pounced, and with super-quick speed and agility, had trussed the crows with the ball of string before Stubbs had whacked them with a duo of stunners. She'd peered around, made sure no one was watching, then twirled them all back to the villa's closet.

"Thanks... I think," Kimi said.

"Aye, thanks," Stella said.

"Don't thank me, thank your father," Stubbs said. "He

had the foresight to prepare us for such an event."

"Don't forget the string thing," Caitlin said, beaming proudly on Stubbs's shoulder.

"Twit!" Emily said from the other shoulder.

"The string was Caitlin's idea," Stubbs said. "If the crows are omens with messages of doom then they can't relay those messages with their beaks tied up. Clever pussy."

Kimi supposed that *was* pretty clever. "Thanks, Cat."

Caitlin mewed.

"Twit!" Emily said again.

"So what happens now?" Rehd said. "What do we do with the crows?"

"Untie them, see what they have to say," Ruthie offered.

"Maybe we should tie rocks round their necks and throw them in the pool," Kimi said. "Dead crows can't talk."

"Aye," Stella agreed.

Stubbs tutted. "You will do no such thing. I will take the crows with me, lock them up until I've had time to think about it. Until then," she turned to Rehd, "as chief of fuzz, dear sir, you need to keep a closer eye on things." Her eyes went to his stomach which was poking over the top of his shorts. "Not least the junk food." With her tulpas still on her shoulders she went to the doors which slid open at a twitch of her nose. "And may I strongly recommend that you do not leave the villa for the remainder of your stay. All of you." She left in a blink and the doors slid shut.

"Crap a crow," Stella said.

"Crap two," Kimi corrected.

"This is bad, isn't it?" Ruthie said. She sidled up to Rehd and clung to him.

"Very," Rehd said. "But I'm sure JJ will deliver."

"What?" Kimi said.

"Donuts. If we can't go out then I'm sure she'll deliver."

Kimi threw a cushion at him which he caught in his teeth. "You don't know, do you?"

Rehd spat the cushion out. "Know what?" By the time they had finished telling of the prawn truck mojo display and the tourist with the camera who had way too much distance between his eyes and a big forehead hidden beneath a cap, Rehd had locked the doors, shuttered all the windows, ordered them to put on their field jackets in case of emergency evacuation, and was now ushering them downstairs to the gym.

The basement gym was the most secure room in the villa, its walls and ceiling embedded with triple layers of Velostat. There was everything they needed for a prolonged stay: shower, toilet, two small rooms with bunk beds, a fridge stocked with pomegranate flavoured Gatorade and tinned foods along with beef jerky for the monkeys; and there was CCTV which covered the rear and front of the villa as well the downstairs living area.

Rehd locked the door and slid the bolts home.

"This is silly," Kimi said. "Don't think I'm staying down here for two days." She climbed onto a vaulting horse, remembered the bubblegum-pink nail varnish, took it out, and began painting her nails. "Last time I'll be able to wear pink."

Ruthie pulled herself up onto the horse. She liked watching Kimi do her nails.

Stella paced the floor.

Rehd got down on a mat and started doing sit-ups.

Ruthie liked the colour so much she asked Kimi to paint hers.

Which she did.

"Bored now," Stella said.

Rehd, now hanging from the wall bars, let go and dropped to the floor. "We have to be safe," he said. "And this is the safest place in the villa."

"But we can't just sit around twiddling our thumbs. We should do something."

"Like?"

"I dunno – what about those crows?"

Rehd stared in thought for a moment. He looked up to Kimi on the horse. "How certain are you it was a walleyed took your picture?"

Kimi thought back. It all happened so fast. Were his eyes too far apart? "I – I – well…"

"You're not certain?"

"I suppose I'm not - not a hundred percent."

"And you?" he turned to Stella.

"I was too busy dragging Kimi away. I remember the guy, but not in detail."

Rehd nodded, turned on his heel and scurried into the computer room. Kimi jumped from the horse and she and Stella and Ruthie followed him inside where he was flicking on the CCTV monitors. The first showed the path outside the villa's front door. Clear. The next showed the living area. Rehd manoeuvred the joystick and the image on screen moved as the camera scanned the kitchen area, the stairs and landing where the twirly room was, the sliding doors that led to the pool – all were clear. The next monitor showed the pool area within the mesh screen. Again – clear.

"Alright then," Rehd said. "There seems to be no immediate threat. I suggest we leave the gym but stay within the house until Balancer Stubbs gets back to us on the crows."

"Sounds good," Stella said. "Kimi?"

Kimi was about to agree when the front doorbell rang, echoing round the gym from the speakers connected to it. They all looked to the first monitor. Balancer Stubbs was at the front door. The camera looked down on her honey-blonde hair. Her shoulders seemed to be moving up and down. She pressed the bell again.

"Is she crying?" Kimi said.

"Aye I think she is," Stella said. "And where's Cat and Em? She never comes over without Cat and Em."

"I don't like this," Rehd said. "It's said some walleyes can shift their shape."

"You're saying there's a greylian at our door? Ach, it looks like Stubbsy to me."

"Not a greylian – a greylian-human hybrid. They can shift their atoms to form a perfect copy, but they can't copy a tulpa."

"Why not?" Kimi asked.

Rehd hissed. "That's beyond my comprendo, Kimi, but I know they can't, and to see Balancer Stubbs without the puss and the birdie, well that gets my hackles up. So we stay calm, and we think this out."

"We should go see." Ruthie scampered away and was sliding the bolts free before anyone else had even moved.

Rehd tutted and ran after her and soon they were all are running up the stairs to the front door. Rehd ordered them back to the sofas. "People, let's be prepared!" he said, then opened the door.

Balancer Stubbs fell inside and dropped to her knees. She wasn't crying at all – she was laughing. She crawled to the sofas and pulled herself up. She flopped herself down, still laughing. Kimi closed the front door, locked it. She'd seen this a few times before, the worst time when Rehd told her the joke about the monkey and the brain. Stubbs had laughed for hours. Now Ruthie was laughing, Stella was starting to giggle. Kimi grinned.

"Remember when I told her the joke about the monkey?" Rehd said, chuckling as he brought a glass of water.

Almost half an hour and a few false starts later Balancer Stubbs finally managed to speak. She told them of her worries, of how, on Kimi's dad's instructions, her and the other Balancers: Cready and Fitstart, had received special training in the treatment of prophetic crows; one of the many angles he'd covered to protect his family. So there she was, with the crows trussed up, unable to speak. She'd watched until they came to, watched them struggle, watched the frustration as they writhed against their bonds, watched until the crows began to cry. They sank to the desk on which they stood and cried, tears streaming down their breasts. At first Alia suspected a trick, but then Emily, wise old bird, suggested undoing the string around the beaks. If either crow had a prophecy for Kimi then Emily surmised it would keep it to itself until it was face to face with Kimi. That made sense. Freeing the beaks would enable some interrogation. So she went to undo the string, but first issued a warning, "I will have you know, crows, I am Balancer Alia Stubbs, soon to be Adept of advanced security. Any trouble from you and my owl will tear your eyes out and my cat will eat them." She freed the knots and the crows opened their beaks. Alia had taken a step back, mojo stirring behind her eyes. Any trouble and the crows would be fried before Em and Cat got to them. She knew that. But the crows did not speak. They laughed.

"Then I untied their wings," Stubbs said. "And I found this clipped under the wing of one, just as they said I would." She smirked and handed a tiny disc to Rehd. "Go on – stick it in and see."

Rehd went to the computer and pushed the little disc into its slot. The screen flickered and Big Sue appeared. He was wearing his tartan dressing gown, and was waving and shouting `yoo-hoo!` The camera spun and Bentley was the one holding the camera. It was the old Bentley, but still, Kimi was pleased to see him. "Hello everyone," he said. "Only two more sleeps for you and we'll be together again." He panned the camera around the room. It was Kimi and Stella's old room, empty, and it was mess. "We're doing the place up for you," he said. "Your room will be perfect when you get here."

"Perfect!" Big Sue said. He whipped a tea towel from his shoulder came up to the camera and polished the lens. The image flickered and the message ended.

"And the other crow?" Rehd said.

Stubbs handed over another disc. Rehd pushed it in the computer. The screen flickered and a greylian appeared.

"Granp!" Stella shouted. "It's Granp!"

The greylian was up close to the camera, black oval eyes glossy with unseen depths. Its slit mouth turned up into the creepy cupcake smile, and despite Granp being Stella's good friend, Kimi's heart began to thud.

"Sssstella, hello," the greylian said. "And Kimi, hello, and Rehd, and Ruthie. Good newsssss…you will not be returning to Heart via twirly…yesssss…I will be bringing you home." Granp smiled again, his eyes blinked twice. "Sssseee you ssssoon!" And the screen went black.

"How cool!" Stella said.

"Very," Ruthie agreed.

"Bentley should have known better than to send crows," Kimi said. "I would have killed them if Balancer Stubbs hadn't stepped in. And anyway, what's so funny?"

"More importantly," Rehd said, "where're your tulpas?"

Stubbs wiped her eyes. "I'm sorry, but when Caitlin realised she'd trussed up messengers bringing you joy and not doom, well, she was mortified. She curled in a ball of embarrassment and refuses to come over here."

"And Emmy?" Stella said. "Where's she?"

"Where do you think Em is?" Stubbs got to her feet. "She's standing over Caitlin `twitting` and `wooing`."

"But it isn't even funny," Kimi said.

Stubbs seemed to ponder this for a while, then said: "Not as funny as the monkey joke, granted, but funny nonetheless."

Everyone was looking at Stubbs.

"Okay, I'm sorry, but when the crows laughed, and Cat got so embarrassed, and Em stood over her calling her a twit until she too started laughing, and -"

"Poor Caitlin," Kimi said.

"Yes, well," Stubbs said. "Perhaps if she had consulted her string idea with me first then it wouldn't have happened. I apologise for my tulpa's behaviour."

"Prove it," Rehd said.

The smile left Stubbs's face. "Prove what?"

"Summon them."

"Cat and Em?"

"Yes, the puss and the birdie. I – I er, I'd like to see they're safe."

Stubbs stared at Rehd for a few long seconds. "You think I would hurt my tulpas?"

"I think I'd like to see them. Just to be sure."

Stubbs snorted.

"Please," Ruthie said. "I'd hate to lose them."

"Yeah," Stella said.

Kimi said nothing. Stubbs's eyes fixed on her.

"What about you, Kimi?"

Kimi nodded.

Stubbs sniffed. "You've all gone mad."

"Failure to comply with a request from the chief of fuzz is an offence," Rehd said.

Stubbs straightened, held her head high, and closed her eyes. A ball of blue mist appeared on her right shoulder and a second later Cat was there in its place.

"Wassup?" Cat said, snuggling at Stubbs's cheek.

More blue mist hung in air above Stubbs's other shoulder, then Emily materialised, apparently asleep. "Twit!" she said, opening one eye.

Stubbs opened hers. "Satisfied?"

Rehd nodded.

"I don't think you are," Stubbs said. "I think you're paranoid, chief of fuzz. Paranoid. And paranoia is contagious and not good for the soul. How dare you think I would harm my tulpas."

Rehd was squirming a little. Kimi could tell because his feet were pawing at each other.

"It wasn't like that," he said.

"Well what exactly was it like?" Stubbs's eyes were wickedly wide. "Is there something I should know?"

You could have a heard a feather drop.

"Something you're not telling me?"

Kimi heard Rehd swallow.

"You're right," he said. "Letting myself get paranoid. I'm sorry, Balancer Stubbs."

Stubbs twitched her nose and the front door unlocked itself and swung open. She left in a blink without another word. The door pulled shut and locked itself.

"Oh deary," Ruthie said.

"Why didn't you tell her about what happened at the shops, about the walleyed?" Kimi asked.

Rehd picked up the remote, pointed and pressed. The doors to the pool slid open. "Because this has all gone too far. There were no crows of doom, only tulpas overreacting. And I'm guessing there's no shape-shifting walleyed cameraman, either. We're all paranoid, that's all."

"So we can go out?" Stella asked.

Rehd thought for a moment. "No," he said. "Pool area, yes, other than that I'm sure we can cope with staying in for two more days. Best to be safe. Now-" he swung the remote to the plasma and *The Little Mermaid* started up again. "Back to business."

They all settled on the sofas. Ruthie made dodo sandwiches. Stella ordered fresh donuts and JJ delivered. Rehd was probably right, Kimi thought. There was no trouble. She smiled at Bentley's stupidity and wondered what their new room would be like. She hoped they'd remember to put a window in the wall. She wondered also about Perry the pot lad. The thought of seeing him again made her heart grow wings. She thought of Charlie Babbage instead, and his clowns. She wondered if he still had them. Then thoughts went to Granp's news. He'd be flying them home in a greylian craft. That would be cool. There was much to look forward to and nothing at all to worry about. On the plasma, Ursula's wedding was about to kick off. Rehd and Ruthie loved this bit, especially the part where the dog bites Ursula's butt. Kimi settled deeper into the cushions and soon the dog was chomping into Ursula and the monkeys were laughing. Kimi was about to join in when she felt a sharp sting at her left elbow. Her hand went straight to it. A small bristly hair poked through. Then a sting to the right elbow. She felt that one – another hair had poked through, hard and bristly. She tucked her arms by her side and said nothing.

"You okay, sister?" Stella asked.

Kimi looked at her. "Fine."

"You sure? No worries?"

Kimi nodded. "No worries."

***

4
EAT ME

When *The Little Mermaid* had finished and Ruthie suggested watching it again, Kimi lied about having a headache and needing an early night. Once locked in the ensuite bathroom she inspected her elbows. A small white needle-like tip poked through the blackened skin at the point of each elbow. She removed her trainers and socks and found the same growing from each heel. She touched the one on her left elbow, which felt hard like the tip of a feather. Her stomach did a little roll and her face ran cold and clammy. Whatever was happening to her would have to wait until she was safely back on Heart. Perhaps then she would tell Mum, or Adept Babbage who she knew she could trust, but nothing was going to stop her from returning. Stella's razor was sitting in its bracket on the shower wall. Kimi ran the hot tap at the sink, took Stella's razor, held her left elbow under the running water, and gently stroked the razor over the protruding white tip. The pain was hot and sharp, worse than squeezing a really bad zit, the blood swirling away down the plughole was way too much. Kimi screamed. She knew there'd be knocks at the door any second.

"Kimi?" It was Rehd.

"Kimi?" now Stella.

"I'm okay." She found Stella's bottle of Styptic Stop and squirted the wound, then shouted something like "YooWooWeeYeeAhhHaaaaaaa!"

"Kimi?"

"I'm okay, I'm okay, I just – just stubbed my toe."

"Twice?" Stella's voice.

"Erm, yeah, silly me."

"Open the door."

Blood spotted the sink, the side, the floor. She sat on the loo. "I'm busy."

"We're making pizza later. You up for some?"

"No thanks. I'm going to bed soon."

"We'll make extra just in case," Rehd said, then footfalls and chatter as they left.

The bleeding had stopped but the thing was still stinging. To do the same to her other elbow, and then to both of her heels was going to hurt like crazy but it had to be done, didn't it? If she turned into a crow in the middle of Florida she might end up in a freak show, or an exhibit in *Ripley's Believe It or Not*. Adept Ripley had given her and Stella a behind-the-scenes tour. Amazing to meet so many adepts. Her mind was wandering now. Then an idea came. If she ran the cold tap instead of the hot, the cold water might numb the area a little, make it less painful. She got to her feet, took a breath, let it out slowly, then approached the sink. She let the cold run for a good time, counted to sixty and realised while doing so that another hour would have passed on Heart. She wondered what Bentley would say right now. She hoped he would be able to get rid of whatever was inside her. She stuck her right elbow under the cold water and held it there. Bentley once drained all the pink from her t-shirt to save her from a bliss fly attack simply by holding her hands. He also drained the pain from her face when she bumped her chin on the dining table. The water was like ice now.

She picked up Stella's razor, rinsed the blood from it, and steadied herself - then spotted Stella's emery boards. She put the razor down, turned the tap off, and dried her elbow, wishing she'd thought of this before.

It worked. The protruding white tip was soon gone, sanded right down to the skin. Her heels, too, were soon as smooth as nature intended. Feeling better about herself she decided she would re-join the others - after all Ruthie's favourite banana and Marmite pizza was always worth a nibble. She washed her face, straightened her clothes, and was about to top up her pink nails when a knock came at the door.

"Kimi, it's me," Stella said. "Stubbs is back. We've got trouble."

"What kind of trouble?"

"Dunno, she won't say until we're all there."

"Okay." Kimi put the nail varnish back in her pocket, stroked concealer over the black spots on her nose, retied her hair, then returned to the living area. Stubbs, all in black with her blonde hair shining - Cat on one shoulder holding a piece of paper in one paw, Emily the owl on the other shoulder holding a piece of paper in her beak - had her hands on her hips and was tapping a foot.

Kimi sat on the couch next to Ruthie. "She looks like she swallowed a wasp," she whispered in Ruthie's ear. Ruthie chuckled.

"Why…" Stubbs began, "…oh why, oh why, oh why… did not one of you think to tell me of your fiasco with the truck?" She looked at each one in turn. "Anyone?"

Silence.

Stubbs looked to Rehd. "*You*, are meant to be the controlling force here. *You* are meant to be in charge. You!" she pointed, "Are responsible for this girl's safety. Why didn't you tell me?"

Rehd got to his feet. "I made a decision, Blondie, a

decision we'll stick to - thank you."

"A poor decision," Stubbs sniffed.

"Let me remind you, sweet lady in black, you are not an adept. Maybe soon, but not yet. Until such times as you can wiggle your nose and make me jump through hoops, I – me – Rehd, chief of fuzz, says what goes down. This is my jurisdiction. Got it?"

Kimi liked it when Rehd got cocky.

Stubbs's face was darkening.

"Hey!" Stella said. "I hope the bad guys aren't on their way while you two are wasting precious time."

"Good point," Stubbs said. She held a palm up to Caitlin and the cat dropped the paper it was holding into it. "This is from Mac." She read from the note: "There's a telephone number for a reporter at CNN. Also the number for a reporter at the local radio station, and the number for a reporter at Fox News, and another for a reporter at the Fortean Times. They all want to see the girl with superhuman strength known as Henrietta Blanche - and last but not least we have the telephone number of Melvin Towser super-rich lawyer to the stars, and father of the little boy you saved. He wishes to shower Henrietta Blanche with gifts and treats beyond her wildest dreams."

"Oh," Rehd said.

"Oh indeed. Mac, of course, has thrown them off the scent, told them he heard Miss Blanche was up from Miami for the day. But they'll soon draw blanks and come back sniffing."

"This isn't good, is it?" Kimi said.

"Isn't good?" Stubbs said. "I've been in touch with my contacts at the press. Henrietta Blanche will appear in every paper tomorrow – and worse still, every paper has received reports within the last hour. She snatched the piece of paper from Emily's beak.

"Twit!" Emily said.

Stubbs read from the paper. "Five sightings of UFOs in the Kissimmee area. Five black cat sightings, five crop circles. It is no wonder you are paranoid, oh great chief of fuzz. You should have told me about this."

"Maybe I should have, but I didn't and now it's done and I can't undo it. I'm sorry, once again. The important thing is what do we do now?"

Stubbs took a deep breath. "We know that some minority greylian groups are after Kimi's head, and we must assume that this unfortunate publicity has brought the attention required to make this no longer a safe-house. Heart is the only safe place for Kimi, and we must evacuate immediately."

Rehd was nodding thoughtfully. Ruthie was picking her teeth. Kimi could feel her shaking. She placed an arm around her just as the light outside faded and wind gusted. Through the glass doors, the small trees against the mesh screen bowed and shook.

"Storm coming," Stella said.

"Yes," Stubbs said. "And we all know how greylian craft can use the elements for disguise. Let's get moving before it's too late." Stubbs ushered them to the stairs. "Kimi and Ruthie and Rehd will go first."

Kimi had a foot on the first step when the sound of the doors to the pool area sliding open made them all stop and turn. A red football bounced in, leaving small wet marks with each bounce, and came to rest at Stubbs's boot. Stubbs twitched her nose and the doors slid together and locked. Rain spots began flicking at the glass, the trees ruffled in the wind and even the surface of the pool was getting choppy. They all remained silent, watching Stubbs as she bent to pick up the ball. "There's someone out there," Stubbs said. "I can feel them."

Cat mewed softly in agreement. Emily stared wide-eyed at the doors.

After what seemed an hour but surely could only have

been five seconds, a small figure stepped into view. The head and face were hidden behind the door's solid centre panel, but through the glass below it was plain to see that it was just a little girl. She wore a white dress tied with a blue bow, the bottoms of blonde ringlets sat on her shoulders. She tapped on the glass.

"It's just a kid," Rehd said. He took the remote from his pocket and pressed it. The doors slid open and the girl stepped inside.

"Hello," she said. "May I have my ball back?"

Kimi went cold. The girl's forehead was a huge white space. Large dark eyes sat almost at the sides of her head.

Stubbs bounced the ball towards the girl and the girl caught it.

"You cooperate well," the girl said. Behind her the pool area grew dark. Rain was coming down hard now. A low grumble of thunder, so close it seemed to send a thrum through the floor. The little girl stepped forward. "Any moment now," she said then gave a bright smile.

"For what?" Stubbs said, and at that moment there was hum in the air like the hum of electricity. The lights inside flickered. There was a low thud and everyone turned to look up the stairs.

"Someone's in the twirly room," Stella said. Blue light was coming from beneath the door. The key in the door was turning. She ran up the stairs, grasped the key and removed it.

"Oh!" the little girl said. "I'm sorry, but you really do need to unlock your closet."

Everyone turned. The girl had somehow snatched Cat from Stubbs's shoulder and was dangling her by the scruff.

"If I don't?" Stella said.

The girl reached behind her back and came back holding a weapon. Kimi recognised it immediately. It was greylian issue, just like the one she'd used to blow a hole in a greylian

General.

"If you don't, your visitor will let himself in anyway. That is unless I roast this stinking cat, first."

There was a bang and a shower of wood splinters which made everyone jump and shriek – apart from the little girl. There was a smoking hole in the closet door where the lock had once been.

"I did warn you," the girl said. The door swung open in a billow of smoke. Everyone backed down the stairs as a slender grey figure emerged from the closet. It wasn't much taller than the little girl, it was stick-thin and had no arm markings like those of the greylian guards. The figure had scars on its arms and legs and a raised ridge of flesh that ran up the right side of its face, puckering one of the eyes so it looked like a crumpled black starfish. The other eye seemed huge in comparison. No one spoke and no one moved as the greylian snaked across the landing to the top of the stairs and looked down at them until its good eye eventually settled on Kimi. It raised its weapon and smiled a familiar cupcake smile. "Yesssss," it said. "That'sss her."

"Oh goody! Everything's in order. I'm pleased," the girl said.

"You wouldn't dare kill Kimi," Rehd said. "You'd start a war."

"Of course she wouldn't kill her," the girl said. "One wrong move and she will blow her foot off."

"That thing is a she?" Stella said. Stubbs shushed her.

The greylian aimed the weapon at Kimi's feet.

"Now for the mathematics," the little girl said. "Let's assume you try something, and my greylian friend puts a stop to it by blowing Kimi's right foot off. Allowing for the other foot and both of her hands, that gives you four wrong moves before we make a start on anyone else's extremities. Do you understand?"

This brought silence. Stubbs looked furious. Helpless and

furious.

"Tell her – tell her you understand," Kimi said to Rehd.

Rehd grunted. "So what now?"

The little girl backed slowly out through the doors. Caitlin dangled from her grip, the weapon pressed against the cat's head.

"Don't try anything, Caitlin," Stubbs said. "That goes for all of you. No one is to be a hero today. I want everyone to do exactly as she asks."

"Fabulous advice," the girl said.

Kimi wanted to pummel her moon-face with stunners. She could see from Stella's look that she felt something similar.

"Why are you doing this?" Stella said.

"I want all of you to come outside and get in the pool," the girl said, moving to one side. "I'm doing this because one should always do good deeds for good rewards. Anyone not in the pool on the count of three and the kitten loses its face. One!"

Kimi went quickly through the doors and jumped into the pool.

Stubbs jumped in too, followed by Rehd and Ruthie. Emily perched on Stubbs's head.

Only Stella remained inside. "What good rewards?" she said.

"Two!" The girl held Caitlin a little further away, closed one eye, tightened her grip on the weapon and pressed it against Cat's cheek. "Join your friends in the pool or I blow the cat to smithereens!" Stella walked through the doors, jumped in the pool. "That was a wise move. I'm delighted," the girl said. She threw Caitlin in the direction of their bobbing heads and she landed softly on Kimi's shoulder.

"Horrible child," Caitlin said quietly.

The girl came to the edge of the pool, and the greylian snaked to her side. "Seeing as I no longer can see your hands and feet, I will train my weapon on the cute owl. My greylian friend here will aim at the monkeys. No funny business, thank you, and you will soon be safely aboard."

The water was warm yet Kimi was shaking. She held onto Stella and found herself wishing for Bentley. She remembered the time in Cohn's lair, freaking out because she had to eat dodo brains, but Bentley heard her anguish and that was enough to bring him to the rescue. It was worth a try, if only she –

"Don't even think about calling your precious tulpa. Make no mistake that I will personally torture any one of you who keeps me from my reward. My lovely, lovely reward."

"What do you get?" Stella said. "What do you get for sending someone to their death? Is the reward worth it?"

"Oh she shan't be going to her death. No. Balancer Kimi Nichols, AKA Henrietta Blanche will be kept alive forever. Her body might go, but her functioning brain will pilot ships through time and space for eternity, or so I'm told. You are very lucky, Kimi. I do so wish it could be me. But alas, I shall be content with my reward."

The greylian by her side smiled and hissed, its shoulders moving up and down in tune with its ugly chuckle. Its puckered eye blinked horribly.

The pattering rain came to a stop, so sudden, as if a giant umbrella had opened up above them. The cloud was thick and as low as the rooftops and some huge, dark thing was rumbling inside it. Kimi held Stella tighter. Stella hugged her back.

"Oh goody, your lift is here," the girl said. A beam of pale light snapped on around them. It made the water sparkle. There was a feeling at the shoulders, as if they were being drawn by a powerful magnet. All at once they began to rise from the pool.

"Keep perfectly still and you will pass through the mesh without too much discomfort," came the little girl's voice.

"Though why I should have told you that I've no idea."

Legs were dangling above the water, all of them dripping wet. "And don't fret about damp clothes. You will dry instantly as you pass onto the ship. I'm just too considerate."

The mesh was approaching. Kimi closed her eyes as it touched her hair, then felt it pass through her with a warm ripple. She opened her eyes as her feet cleared the mesh. Everyone was clinging to everyone else, looking up into the cloud where the dark shape lurked, apart from Stella. "What's your reward?" she shouted to the girl below.

The girl put her hands to her grinning mouth to make herself heard, "One hundred billion American dollars. It's a very respectable reward. My best ever."

Stella whistled at this.

Kimi spoke up, "Why take all of us if it's just me you want? Let them go. Take me and I'll do whatever you want."

The girl laughed. "Don't be such a cliché. It doesn't become you. Fear not, your friends aren't going far. They'll be dropped in a desert somewhere. I'm sure they'll be able to choose if they ask nicely. Which one do you fancy? The Gobi? The Sahara? Or perhaps the Kalahari, one of my personal favourites."

"You're disgusting as well as stupid," Stubbs said.

"Agreed," whimpered Ruthie.

"Eat me!" The girl was waving.

"Almost a year in hiding and I'm dobbed in by a kid. A walleyed kid," Kimi said.

They were a few metres above the mesh screen, and in line with the roof of the villa, when the magnetic pull suddenly ceased and they all dropped heavily to the mesh below – apart from Emily who instinctively thrashed her wings and stayed in the air. The mesh sunk, buckled, threatened to collapse. Kimi landed on her feet and fell to her knees. Her right knee tore the mesh from its seam. She pulled back quickly, and through the hole in the mesh saw the little girl looking puzzled by this sudden change of events, the greylian next to her more so. Both of them raised their weapons. There was no thinking in what Kimi did next. It was instinctive, like Emily thrashing her wings. Perhaps it was that which made Kimi act without hesitation, helped along by her earlier wish to thump Moonface, but whatever it was, she found herself gazing in awe at the perfect silvery stunners forming at her wrist and loading themselves into the grooves of Little Hand, whirling themselves around the rifled grooves and out from the pointed tips of her fingers directly through the hole in the mesh. Moonface's expansive forehead was taking a pummelling, as was the ugly greylian. They both dropped their weapons and staggered helplessly. Stella was laughing, and that made Stubbs laugh too. Ruthie and Rehd were clapping, all of them balancing on the mesh which was only just holding and threatening to buckle under their weight.

The little girl slipped, grabbed the greylian to save herself and they both splashed into the pool. Someone said something about getting down - it might have been Caitlin - when the air hummed and the pull jerked them upright. They were being lifted once again, but faster than before. Before Kimi could blink, she was dry, strapped to some kind of bed, and staring at a metallic ceiling with a single circular window in its middle where clouds soon cleared and pinprick stars went gliding by.

***

5
Area 51

A low hum pervaded the warm room. A strap across Kimi's forehead prevented movement, but she could see from the corners of her eyes that she was with the others, all of them strapped to tables in what appeared to be a circular arrangement.

"Everyone here, everyone okay?" It was Stubbs.

Everyone piped up. All present and accounted for.

"Wowee!" Ruthie's voice. "I see stars. We're in space. Monkeys in space. Space monkeys!"

"Yes we are." Stubbs's voice. "Oh my gosh look at that!" Through the circular window in the ceiling, a huge globe had slid into view. It was growing bigger by the second. "That's our Earth. Isn't it beautiful?" Stubbs again.

"What's happening?" Kimi said.

"We're going in," Stubbs said as Earth came up to meet the window. They were heading for a vast brown area, in the middle of which sat a white splodge.

"Is that a desert?" Stella's voice. "Like the kid said?"

"It's desert alright," Stubbs said. "The Nevada Desert to be precise."

The white splodge was coming closer. "We're going into

a lake?" Kimi said.

"No," Stubbs said. "Well, yes and no. It's a lake, but a lake made of salt, not water. At least that's what people think. But really, we're heading for Earth's largest portal to Heart – Area 51!"

Kimi felt her stomach turn over, which was a weird feeling seeing as she could feel little of her own body. Obviously they were in space – no gravity. As the white splodge filled the window and wisps of cloud whipped past, Kimi's stomach rolled again. Not wanting to puke into the weightless air she closed her eyes and held her breath. Feeling – or gravity – was returning, pulling against the straps holding her to the table.

"We're going in!" Rehd's voice.

"Amazing!" Stubbs's voice.

"Wow!" Stella's voice.

"Meweweweww," Caitlin's shaky voice.

"Woo!" said Emily.

"I think I'm going to pee myself," Ruthie's voice.

Kimi kept her eyes tightly closed. A ferocious rattle, deafening, like hailstones, followed a swooping feeling in the gut that made them all groan and moan. And then silence, and that feeling of being unable to move. Kimi opened her eyes. The window showed only darkness. The table she was strapped to was tilting forward. From the corners of her eyes she could see the tables either side, Stubbs on one, Stella on the other, also tilting forward. Blue light appeared below and Kimi began to slide from the table as the strappings around her legs, chest and forehead, vanished. She closed her eyes again.

…and opened them once more to bright lights and a monkey's face. A monkey with spectacles and a big smile. "You are safe, Kimi Nichols," the monkey said. "I'm Lucy. Welcome to Area 51."

Kimi sat up. Some thirty feet above her, and bigger than

a house, a dull grey saucer-shaped craft hung silently in the air. They appeared to be in some kind of enormous cavern. Rows upon rows of hovering craft, some saucer-shaped, some shaped like tear drops, and others triangular, black and dart-like, filled the air above white cabins which Kimi guessed were offices or laboratories. Lots of important-looking people milled around, mingling with greylians and monkeys. They seemed unfazed by the appearance of Kimi and the others, their chatter happy and busy and interspersed with laughter.

"Don't be worried," the monkey said. She had a voice that was soft and warm and she stood taller than any monkey Kimi had ever seen. She also wore a ladybird hairclip which kept her fringe pinned back. "No one here knows we have important guests." Soft honey-coloured fur shone around her face and neck and disappeared into a white coat. She was holding what looked like an iPad. It had ladybird stickers on the back. A blue badge on her coat pocket said *Lucy – here to help*.

"Hi. And er, thanks," Kimi said.

"Ah!" Lucy said. "Here's Granp. Your knight in shining spaceship."

"Granp?"

Granp's slender grey figure skated wraithlike through the crowds of people. Kimi almost died of surprise when he greeted Lucy with a kiss on each cheek. "Hello again," he said, to Kimi then gave that cupcake smile that always made her stomach squirm.

"Shall we wake your friends?" Lucy smiled, waited.

Kimi looked around. Arranged in a circle were tables similar to those they had been strapped to in the craft. Stubbs was snoring. Rehd and Ruthie motionless. Stella's mouth was open. Caitlin was in a ball, and Emily had her head buried in her chest. "Er, yes please."

Lucy pressed something on her iPad which woke the

others in an instant. After only a few moments, Lucy had walked around the tables, introduced herself, and had them all lined up before her – Kimi included.

With Granp by her side, she began: "Ladies, fellow simians, gorgeous owls and lovely pussycats." She screwed her button nose up and smiled and placed a paw on Granp's bony shoulder. "Granp has had you under surveillance for some time, and -"

"For some time?" Stubbs said. "How the heck didn't we know about this?"

Lucy pushed her specs up her nose and stared at Stubbs. "The powers that be preferred discretion, Balancer Stubbs. And be it known, their preference for discretion was no reflection on your more than proficient capabilities. Security is always at its best when discreet, I am sure you will agree."

"Isn't it better to share? If we're all on the same page we stand a better chance."

Lucy held up a paw. "I'm sorry, Balancer Stubbs. Discussing security matters with me would really be a waste of time. I have no say. I am here solely to debrief you and help you on your way. So if you wouldn't mind saving any queries regarding mission security and addressing them to the Adepts at a later time? Then we can get on with what we're here for."

"Fair enough," Stubbs said.

"As I was saying," Lucy continued, "Granp had you under his watchful eye, spotted the bounty hunter in the form of the little girl, saw the attempted abduction, and skilfully intervened." She tucked the iPad under her arm and started clapping.

While the others joined in and gave thank yous, Stella ran up and kissed Granp on the cheekbone. Granp wrapped his skinny, rubbery arms around her and lifted her up in a hug. Kimi thought she might be sick.

"So that's why the pull stopped and we dropped onto the

mesh," Stubbs said.

"Yesssss," Granp said, releasing Stella and smiling his cupcake smile.

"That's right," Lucy said. "You were within fifty metres of boarding an old cruiser. Granp slipped his smaller ship in underneath the cruiser, cut off their abduction beam – that's when you landed on the mesh roof – then he engaged his own beam and flew you away before the pilot of the cruiser knew what had hit him." She patted Granp on the back.

"So we're safe." Ruthie scampered over to Granp, took his hands, leapt into his arms, and planted a kiss on his slit mouth. Granp looked shocked as she scampered back to the line.

Rehd sighed and muttered *"Monkey see, monkey do,"* under his breath.

"Here are your instructions..." Lucy studied the iPad. "Balancer Stubbs and tulpas Caitlin and Emily will return, along with Granp, to the villa. You will clean up, lock up, and ensure all possessions are returned to Heart as quickly as possible. Are we clear?"

"Clear," said Stubbs.

"Twit," Emily said.

Cat nodded.

"That's good. Now, where was I, oh yes, chief Rehd, you and your lovely wife will leave immediately for Heart where you are to be briefed on security for Kimi's return."

"How long 'til Kimi returns?" Rehd asked.

"She will leave in one hour. The time difference will give you sixty hours to ensure Kimi's arrival is risk free."

"Sounds good," Rehd said.

Stella raised a hand. "What about me?"

"You will wait and travel with Kimi," Lucy said. "You are still her mentor, after all."

The others were dismissed. There were hugs all round and plenty of kisses and Kimi had to hold back the tears while saying goodbye to Cat and Em. "We shall all be fine," Stubbs reassured. "And we'll see you again soon enough." And soon enough they were gone, back into the craft and slipping through the rocky ceiling with Granp. And then came more tears as Ruthie and Rehd were led away for transportation.

"Let's do a final check," Lucy said. She looked Kimi and Stella up and down. Her eyes hovered over Kimi's old jacket, or rather, Stella's old jacket that she had given to Kimi. Red leather, heavily scuffed and scratched, buckles missing here and there, and no arms. "We can fix you up with a new jacket before you go."

"No thanks," Kimi said. "I like this one."

Lucy raised an eyebrow, then took Kimi's hand and examined the pink nail varnish. "Bliss flies are hungry this time of year," she said. "Best if you go and scrub that off. She let go of Kimi's hand. "You will find everything you need there." She indicated the nearest white cabin. A sign on the door said GATE 13. "Go relax, freshen up, and Heart will be ready for you in about an hour."

Inside the cabin the main waiting area held five small round tables with mesh chairs. The place was empty. There were vending machines for tea, coffee, pommy juice, and one filled with crisps and chocolate bars; all were set to free vend. On one wall were toilets marked HUMAN MALE and HUMAN FEMALE. On another wall more toilets: MONKEYS, and GREYLIANS. "What the heck do you think greylians do to go to the loo?" Kimi said.

Stella shrugged. "Let's go investigate."

Kimi declined, nodded to a final door, this one marked GATE TO HEART. Someone had scrawled underneath in felt pen `Heart is where the Home is`

"Not long now," Kimi said.

"You nervous?"

"A little," Kimi said. "It's been a long time."

"What are you looking forward to the most?" Stella

helped herself to a pack of Reese's Peanut Butter Cups from the vending machine. "Want one?"

"No thanks. I feel a bit sick after flying to the moon and back."

Stella pressed the button for two more packs and shoved them in her jacket.

"The famoose - come to think of it."

"What?"

"Looking forward to seeing them. I mean, I love Bentley…"

"Everyone loves Mr B," Stella said.

"…and I'm looking forward to seeing Big Sue. And Charlie. Yes, I really can't wait to see Charlie again."

"Aren't you forgetting someone?"

Kimi felt her cheeks warming. She turned towards the toilets. "Yes," she said. "Mr Purse. I need some new pull-in pants."

"You know who I mean," Stella said, following Kimi into the toilets.

Kimi stared at herself in the mirror. "Apparently, jumping in a pool during a downpour, being drawn through mesh by an alien abduction beam, and tumbling through space with no gravity, can make one's concealer vanish from one's nose."

Stella was at her side, peering at Kimi's reflection. "Those black spots have grown."

In a cabinet to the side of the mirror, Kimi found some nail varnish remover. Ten bottles of the stuff. Pink-tainted cotton pads in the waste basket, lots of them, along with at least three discarded bottles of pink nail varnish that she could see, made her smile as she imagined how many Balancers and how many Adepts had scrubbed their pink nail varnish away before transporting back to the crazy world of Heart where bliss flies devoured pink, crows flew in swarms, and dodo was the dish of the day. She smiled at herself in the mirror.

"Bet I know who you're thinking of," Stella said.

Kimi watched her cheeks turn red. She ran the cold tap and splashed her face.

"Would you kiss him?"

Kimi soaked a pad with nail varnish remover and started wiping at her nails. "Hate bliss flies." She remembered the taxidermy display that Stella had done; a Bellamy's Aunt with a bliss fly, white and plump and big as a fist, its long pink probe screwed into the toad's tongue. All shiny with varnish and arranged nicely under a glass dome. She half hoped it might have been destroyed when her jump through time and space sent the green mount sliding down on Middling. She scrubbed harder.

"I asked you a question."

Kimi looked once more in the mirror. Bright, nervous eyes stared back.

"What about your elbows?"

Kimi rolled up a sleeve. The skin was dark, cracked, the small bristle showing once again.

"And your heels?"

"Same." Kimi continued scrubbing, got every last particle of pink away, took the nail varnish bottle from her breast pocket, and slung it in the bin.

"You don't look well." Stella retrieved the nail varnish from the bin and pushed the bottle back into Kimi's pocket. "Waste not want not."

"What's the point? I can't use it."

"We could get leave or a mission at any time, Kimi. You might even get a date. Be prepared and all that."

"It's only a bottle of nail varnish. I can buy a new one any time I want." She went to remove the bottle from her pocket.

Stella grabbed her hand. "You really should keep it."

Stella looked tense, or was it stern? Stella didn't usually

do stern. "You're freaking me out. It's a bottle of nail varnish. What does it matter?" Kimi turned to back to the mirror, away from Stella's glare.

"You can be such an arse, Kimi. One day it might come in handy, then you would regret throwing it away. Can't you see that?"

Kimi felt the urge to shove Stella up against the wall. The air between them appeared thick and charged, as if they both might attack each other any second.

"You know I'm talking sense," Stella said.

"You sound like my mother."

"Your mother is a star!"

"What?"

"And as for your dad, he's precious, and priceless."

Kimi was lost for words.

"You should be grateful, and thankful, and look after what you've got."

"What do you mean what I've got? What I've got is…"

"What you've got…" Stella took a step closer. "…is everything every kid wishes they could have."

"You've gone nuts."

Stella shook her head. "Not nuts, Kimi. I just know what I'm talking about."

"Where's Stella gone?"

"Stella is here, and might I remind you that I am your mentor, and that means you listen to my wisdom."

"Yep – nuts!" Kimi retrieved the nail varnish from her breast pocket and lobbed it once more into the waste bin.

Stella reached for the bottle, stared at the label, "Bubblegum Pink - perfect!" shoved it back into Kimi's pocket, threaded the strap through the buckle, pulled it tight, then placed a hand on Kimi's shoulder. "Wisdom," she said, solemnly, then: "Wisdom is the food of the fishes! Listen to it!"

"What in the blazing heck are you…"

A tap on the door.

Lucy's bright face peered in. "Ready when you are."

"Wow," Stella said. "This is it, Kimi, we're really going home. Come on, hero!" She patted Kimi on the back as she passed, and the door swung shut as she left.

Kimi took one last look in the mirror. There was something she could feel but couldn't pin down. As if perhaps the person looking back was not her. How could she be labelled a hero? Kimi Nichols, a kid from Mousehole with a dodgy hand who seemed to be turning into a crow. The image in the mirror morphed into beautifulness. Perry smiled back at her. His wild hair, smooth chocolate complexion, and white smile made her heart patter. She closed her eyes, heard the door open behind her.

"Kimi?" It was Stella.

"Give me one more minute."

"You okay?"

"Yes, just one minute. Please."

The door swung shut.

When she opened her eyes, Perry had gone. The girl that stared back, with straggles of dyed blonde hair, with skin as pallid as death, did not look like Kimi Nichols; this girl looked ready to snarl, to bite. The fluorescent lights flickered, buzzed. She took the nail varnish from her pocket and, without taking her eyes off her reflection, lobbed it in the direction of the bin. She heard it land next to another bottle with a clink. She closed her eyes once more, wanting everything to settle into its rightful place. She counted to ten then left the toilet, but even as she walked back into the waiting room the door bumped her back and she was overwhelmed by a feeling of faintness. She immediately sat down and Lucy made a fuss, insisting on a sweet cup of tea and a biscuit before being allowed to travel. Kimi drank the tea gratefully, but only managed a nibble of the biscuit. The feeling of discomfort had gone. Mum had told her that some places have cold spots, and those were places to stay away from. Just like the toilets back in Mousehole school, the toilets here were not a nice place to be. Stella had gone all weird, too. Kimi decided this was possibly the biggest discombobulation she had ever experienced. Probably the abduction beams. Bentley once told her that abduction could be a painful process.

After gentle encouragement and a reminder from Lucy that the clock was ticking and that for every minute they were late they would be keeping their tulpas waiting for another hour, Kimi agreed she was feeling well enough to twirly. Stella whooped and slapped her five. *She* seemed to be back to her old self, too. Kimi decided not to mention the discarded nail varnish.

They followed Lucy through the door marked 'GATE TO HEART' and stepped into a room the size of a football pitch. Lucy went to a podium that held a control panel and began pressing buttons. A column of light as thin as a pencil and stretching from the floor to the ceiling appeared a few metres in front of the podium. "This is the latest in twirly technology. We can transport you to anywhere in this world, or on Heart, to within one centimetre tolerance."

"That's a twirly?" Stella said.

"Oh yes," Lucy smiled. "It also has built in fizzle diffusers so you don't get too much of that crazy feeling when your atoms separate."

"Can we just get on with it? Please." Despite the fact that she had practised twirling in the gym every day, Kimi was not yet used to twirlies, and that fizzling sensation was unpleasant to say the least. Then a staggering thought came; what about her nose, her elbows, those things on her heels, what if the twirly took her apart but put her back together again as a crow? Her mouth went dry.

Stella's hand took hers, squeezed. "You still haven't answered my question," she whispered.

"Huh?" Kimi was breathing hard.

"Now, girls, coordinates are set to take you to your room at the Rabbit's Foot. Your tulpas await you." Lucy smiled.

"Kiss him, would you kiss him?"

"On five, you will please step into the wind. Thank you. Four!"

"There's wind?" Stella said.

"Yes," Lucy said. "Look closely and you'll see. When you step into the beam it will engulf you quite pleasantly."

"I'm worried," Kimi said. "Buffers or not, what if I turn into a…"

"…and three!"

"Ach you'll be fine."

"…and two!"

"Wait!" Kimi said.

"One!" Lucy said. And at that moment Stella stepped forward and dragged Kimi with her.

The light spread around them in a flash, the fizzling began.

***

6
A Hero's Welcome

The old red leather of Kimi's jacket started to fill with holes. Particles peeled away into the air before vanishing. She lifted Little Hand, watched it disintegrate. Her vision blurred, fogged, then cleared with a hiss and she was staring at a Bellamy's Aunt with a bliss fly attached to its tongue.

"That was quick," Stella said.

Kimi laughed. Not at Stella, but at the snoring heaps on the two brand new four-poster beds. The bed on the right had tartan drapes. On it lay Big Sue, his legs hanging over the end, feet touching the floor. On the left, where Kimi had once cried herself to sleep on a tatty old camp bed, stood the other four-poster with purple drapes. And there lay Bentley, not the old Bentley Kimi had expected, but the tiny five-year-old version, curled up and sleeping peacefully. A round table with three wooden chairs took up the floor space between the beds.

Big Sue stirred. He opened one eye and grinned through his beard when he saw the two of them and then he hooted – which woke Bentley.

Big Sue hugged Stella then Kimi. Kimi hugged Bentley. Stella kissed Bentley on the cheek and tweaked his little nose, at which Bentley shuddered and expanded into the old Bentley who seemed a lot more wrinkly than Kimi recalled. "I – erm, I have developed a habit for sleeping in my child form," he said. "I wake up much chirpier. Anyway, you took your bloomin time."

"Sorry," Kimi said. "Wasn't feeling too good."

"That's alright, deary," Big Sue said. "I quite enjoyed my nap."

"What's that?" Stella pointed to the wall at the end of the room where thick red curtains hung.

Bentley ran to the curtains and pulled a cord. They swished open and sunlight burst through a six-paned window. "Your wish was my command."

Big Sue coughed. "Our command."

"Yes, of course. And what's more you've started a fashion. Everyone is fitting new windows in their spires."

"That's cool. Looks nice outside," Kimi said. "Can we go out?"

"It's nice but nippy," Bentley said. "And of course you can go out. You're going on a little tour."

"Of what?" Stella said, gazing around their freshly decorated room.

"Not you, Stella," Big Sue said. "You can stay with me and I'll fill you in. Bentley has orders to show Kimi a few things, before..."

"Before the celebrations," Bentley cut in. "Now, how do you want me?" he asked Kimi.

"Medium," Kimi said with no hesitation.

"Around your age?"

"Two years older. Please."

Bentley's face screwed up. He shuddered violently, his wrinkled features smoothed and he shrank to a boy resembling a good imitation of a grinning fourteen year-old. "That do?"

"Perfect," Kimi said. "But what's this tour? I'm not sure I

want to see anyone."

Big Sue came over, whipped a tea towel from his shoulder and started dusting down Kimi's jacket. "I had hoped you would have burnt this smelly old thing a long time since," he said. "But don't worry, put a brush through your hair and you'll be right as rain. The people will be fine. You're quite the hero don't you know." He sniffed and there was a glint of a tear in his eye.

"That's right," Bentley said. "Quite the hero. Shall we be off?" He raised a finger and began to whisk the air.

Kimi grabbed his wrist. "Can we walk instead?"

Bentley hesitated, then brightened. "Of course. But we'll need to speed it up. There's sort of a schedule."

"Schedule?"

"Yes."

"Can I get away with not going?"

"Erm, no, sorry, no can do," Bentley said. "Listen, this'll be fun. You must be proud of who you are, Kimi. What you did was an amazing accomplishment. There aren't many folks who can claim to have changed time and saved thousands of lives in the process."

"Aye," Stella said. "You get off with Mr B and have some cosy time. You deserve it."

Kimi said to Big Sue, "You don't look too happy about it."

Big Sue's huge arm wrapped itself around Stella and pulled her into his stomach. "Don't mind me, dear. I'm an old wet so and so, really. I'm just happy we're all back together, at the Foot, where we belong." He blew his nose on a tea towel. "But I'll be much happier after tomorrow is done with."

"What about tomorrow?"

"Alright." Bentley opened the door. "We need to go."

"Bathroom first," Kimi said.

Stella followed Kimi into the bathroom. Kimi rolled her sleeves up. The bristles on her elbows had grown, each a few centimetres long; the skin they sprouted from was black and cracked. Kimi found an emery board and began to file them away.

"I'm sensing you're not happy," Stella said.

Kimi did not reply until the bristles were gone. She rolled her sleeves down and kicked off her shoes. "Course I'm not happy." She peeled down her sock. The bristle coming from her heel was bent downwards; the skin around it darkened and cracked. "I'm a freak. Would you be happy if you were turning into a hedgehog?" She kicked off the other shoe, sat on the loo, and used the emery board to remove the bristles.

"Brought you this." Stella lobbed her a tube of concealer. "The spots on your nose need covering up."

The black marks had spread to an ovular shape, each about one centimetre long. Kimi inspected them for bristles, felt for them with a finger. There were none. "What do you think they are?"

"Dunno. Maybe we should tell Bentley. Get you to the doc's."

Kimi stared at the black ovals. They reminded her of greylian eyes, and also of a bird's nostrils. Something was inside her. Something wanting out. "I don't know what to do."

A rap on the door made Kimi jump.

"Kimi?" It was Bentley.

"Be there in a minute, Mr B!" Stella's hand came on Kimi's shoulder. "Let's get today out of the way. This is all new. Go with Bentley, he obviously has some things to show you."

"But why just me? And why's Big Sue acting all weird."

"I guess we'll find out soon enough. Look, Kimi, go with the flow for now and have some fun. We'll discuss it tonight."

"Fun?"

"Yes, fun." Stella slapped her on the back.

*

Downstairs, the bar area was empty apart from Bentley who sat by the door. The place was gleaming; tables and stools polished, floor shiny, and the frosted glass partitions separating the cubicles sparkled from the sunlight angling through the windows. Bentley got up, smiled. "Later, after your tour, we will be having a little celebratory feast in your honour. Just friends and family."

"Where is Mum and Dad?" Kimi asked, suddenly remembering she had parents.

"Ah," Bentley opened the door. "They're on our schedule." He stood aside to let her pass.

"What is it you're not telling me this time?"

Bentley's smile dropped. "I'm doing what I've been ordered to do. Can I ask that you at least try and appreciate that and humour your old tulpa?"

Kimi stepped outside. Her parents' house stood tall and bright in the sunlight. The painting of her great-great grandfather on the front of the house had faded badly. A dozen or so people going about their business soon had their eyes on Kimi. One man in a thick coat came over and shook her hand. "Grand job," he said. "Pleasure to make your acquaintance."

"Well done, Miss Nichols," a woman shouted.

A young boy stepped up, bowed. "Thank you for saving my family," he said.

Kimi flustered some acknowledgements, looked to Bentley.

Bentley shrugged. "Should have done this by twirly."

Kimi took his hand. "Get me out of here."

One twirled finger later and they arrived on Karnaby Street, right outside BoZone. Mr Purse, still with his bent nose, spectacles and big quiff of hair was standing in the doorway. He gave a silent round of applause before raising both arms and then bowing so low that his fingers almost touched the floor. "I'm so delightfully charmed to see you again," he said on returning upright.

Kimi felt her cheeks warming. Someone passing shouted "well done" another "thank you" another "you're our hero" and Kimi wanted the ground to swallow her up.

"We have a new jacket," Mr Purse said. "Designed in your honour. It's an adorable duck egg blue. And it's called, quite simply and with delirious artistry: *Time*! Isn't that awesome?" he grinned and bounced on his heels.

"Awesome," Kimi said.

"And here," he dipped in his pocket and pulled out a silver necklace with a small crow pendant. "From me to you. A thank you gift. May I?"

Kimi stepped forward, lowered her head. Mr Purse fastened the necklace in place, Kimi thanked him, examined the little silver crow. "That's very neat."

"And!" Mr Purse tapped his nose. "We have a whole new range of tees, jeans, and boots which will be unveiled tomorrow, when you will be given the choice of absolutely anything you want." He clasped his hands together and held them to his nose. "I'm so proud of you, you know. So proud."

"Thanks very much," Kimi said. She looked to Bentley… *Weird* she thought, and Bentley raised an eyebrow before whisking the air once again.

Now they were in Pommy Wood, tucked behind one of the house-sized standing stones. Forty two of these ran the circumference of the wood and they had fallen like dominoes when Kimi had used their power to transfer through time and dimensions, but now they were upright again and across their tops huge slabs of rock kept them in place.

"Precautions," Bentley said. "Should anyone else ever abuse their powers round here, at least they won't topple."

"Right," Kimi said, then spotted an old friend. A

famoose, its wings shimmering as it leapt from bramble to bramble. More famoose appeared, coming through the trees as glowing spheres, the fast-moving wings whirring and clicking brought back memories of the famoose dome frapping at the crows.

Soon they were surrounded, one hundred - two hundred? One hovering sphere came gliding right up to Kimi's face. She held out her palm and the famoose lowered to it, stopped whirring. Wings unfolded and the grey rodent looked at her with its fierce red eyes. "Hero!" it said, before leaping to the air in tittering giggles. Whispers of "hero – hero" came from the gathered famoose as they played and swam in the air.

Kimi sighed.

"You're famous," Bentley said, twirling the air once more.

Now they were at the clearing in the centre of Pommy Wood. The old Shed was there, dusty and ramshackle and looking as if it might topple if touched. The faded sign on the door was still there,

THE
Scholarium for Harmonious Extrasensory Development
sitvis vobiscum

"You said the Shed got flattened," Kimi said.

"It did, this is the new one," Bentley said.

The door swung open. Rehd stepped out. His hair looked freshly cut and he was dressed in the same camouflage gear he'd worn on the day time turned inside out. His face lit up when he saw Kimi. She ran to him, hugged him. "Good to see you, Kimi," he said. "Glad to be back in the land of plenty?"

"Yeah. Where's Ruthie?"

"Oh you know, she's at home pruning the roses." Rehd remained standing in the doorway.

"Aren't we going in? Or down? Or whatever it is," Kimi asked.

"Not right now," Rehd said. "There's erm, well, you're not allowed, not until -"

"Tomorrow?" Kimi finished for him.

"Yes, tomorrow."

"I hope you lot aren't planning a surprise party," Kimi said. "I hate surprises."

Rehd looked at the sky. "Nice day again. Bit chilly though."

"Time to go," Bentley said. He took Kimi's hand and the air spun around her.

Now they were on the outskirts of Middling, behind the streets where the dodo farm stood resplendent, much bigger than before, and behind it the vast mountain - which Kimi had last seen revealed as a pyramid when its coat of mud and grass slid from its sides - was a green mountain once again.

"They had to recreate the dodos after the landslide killed the stock," Bentley said. "But I must say the new version is even tastier."

"Don't tell me," Kimi said. "I can try some tomorrow?"

Bentley didn't get to reply. A small door opened at the side of the building. Two people came out, deep in conversation. An older man in a smart suit had an arm on the shoulder of a boy dressed in blue overalls. Kimi recognised the spiky hair and immediately felt her cheeks flushing. Perry looked up, smiled his white smile. "Kimi!"

The man in the suit smiled, too. Kimi thought she recognised him from somewhere. He came rushing over, clasped her by the shoulders and planted a kiss on her forehead. "I owe you my life," he said. "And I know that's a small thing compared to the many thousands you undoubtedly saved, Kimi, but really, I never thought such happiness could exist for me. Not ever again. Look at me, look at what you have done for me, and for Perry, too. The people of Middling are positively brimming with gratitude."

"Let me explain," Bentley said. "You might remember Barry. Apparently you pinged his sabre on the day of your last mission."

Kimi remembered. Of course. This was the man who wore only a sack. He'd lost his mojo and relied on donations. Kimi had almost blown up his organ. "Hi," she said.

"I can't thank you enough," Barry said. "With my newfound mojo I became the inventor I once was. Between Perry and myself, the dodos were resurrected, and not only do we have new and improved dodos, but we have the sweetest machinery in place – automatic conveyors and hoppers. The dodos are fed and watered and their poop scooped and recycled. All we have to do is fill and empty the hoppers thrice a day."

"Well that's great," Kimi said.

Perry said, "Perhaps I can show you around… erm…"

"Tomorrow?" Kimi said.

"Actually I was going to say this afternoon. I can show you how everything works." Then he added in a weird attempt at a creepy voice, *"How a hero's mojo works in mysterious ways."*

Kimi didn't understand what he meant, so she just smiled and nodded.

Barry looked at his watch. It was silver and sparkled with what looked like diamonds. "I have to nip to BoZone," he said. "Mr Purse has made me some pterodactyl skin shoes. I'll see you all later. And thank you again, Kimi. It's so lovely to see you again." He twirled his finger and vanished. Then Perry winked and did the same.

"Pterodactyl shoes?" Kimi turned to Bentley.

"Oh yes," Bentley said. "You might recall, some of the

old birds were killed when you er, when the black mount erupted. Well, nothing wasted. The skin is tough and durable and lasts for years. Mr Purse is looking into genetically engineering the same."

"Right," Kimi said. All she could think of was Perry's white smile.

"Don't you think this is all amazing? Lives saved and advances made."

"How come there's no greylians hanging around?"

"Ah!"

"Ah what?"

"There's a partial ban."

"Partial?"

"Yes, well, they have to park their craft outside of Middling and must have clearance before being allowed to mingle or use Middling's facilities."

"Because of me, right?"

Bentley hesitated. Kimi felt an invisible barrier, like a breeze. Then it lifted as Bentley continued: "No," he said, "Not because of you; because some greylians, given half a chance, would take you from us." Bentley stared up into space and sighed. "Who knows how far you would travel before…"

A crow cawed, Little Hand gave a harsh tingle. Kimi swore and shook the tingles away. "Before what?"

Bentley swallowed. "Before they divided your brain into a million pieces and used you to pilot entire fleets through time and space."

The sun slipped behind a cloud. Kimi flexed Little Hand as far as its binding scars would allow. Her brow throbbed. Golden sparkles of mojo circled her wrist.

"You should be extremely proud, Kimi. What you did was braver than brave, and everyone in Middling knows it and appreciates it. There's a price on your head, yes, but you have your friends – and me, of course – to protect you."

"I'm sick of this tour."

It started to rain a fine cold drizzle.

Bentley shuddered, expanded, and the old Bentley raised a finger. "One last stop!"

Now they were at the wall outside the library looking down on Middling. "I think I need a lie down," Kimi said. "I can feel a headache coming on."

"It's all the excitement, that's all it is."

"Excitement? And why have you changed to old Bentley. I like you better as a boy."

"Haven't lost your charm, have you? We're here to see Patina. She has important news, and for that I must look my most respectable."

"What news?" Kimi followed Bentley through the small blue door.

"Lights!" he yelled. High on the ceiling a pumpkin light blinked to life, and as they walked through the aisles of books, more pumpkin lights on the ceiling woke up, lighting the way.

Kimi grabbed Bentley's elbow just before they reached the small door in the back wall. "What news?"

Bentley stared at her. "I tried to get out of this you know. I knew I'd mess things up."

"What have you messed up?"

"Well, look at you, all miserable. The tour was supposed to perk you up, give you confidence for -" He stopped abruptly and turned to the door.

Kimi grabbed him again. "Confidence for what?"

"Trust me, Kimi... you are about to find out."

He opened the door and stepped into the light.

*

Kimi followed Bentley's silhouette through the yellow light and into the immense library. Polished marble chequered the floor in white and green. A hundred or more desks stood in rows, and, sitting at them with heads down and scribbling furiously, were the blonde-haired secretaries in their yellow jumpers. They all looked up at once, smiled, pushed their spectacles up their noses, then looked back down again, hissing in whispers. Tall chrome columns stood on either side of the vast room and ran in pairs into the distance. Between the columns, shelves upon shelves holding millions of books, and above, through oval shaped holes in the ceiling, the arrangement repeated over and over. Once again Kimi had the feeling of being swallowed by a whale.

"You all right?"

Kimi nodded. "Yeah, look…" The wispy form of Patina was sweeping towards them; resplendent, back arched, head high and wearing the most hideous flowery gown in green and purple which trailed the floor for twenty metres behind her. She stopped somewhere near the middle of the rows of desks, the secretaries now silent but still working feverishly. Patina bent down and came back up holding the hem of her gown. "Girls, you are dismissed," she said. The secretaries all left their desks at once, dissolved into yellow light, and shot up Patina's skirt. Silence.

"This way, guys," Patina said. She swished around and glided across the marble floor with only the whisper of her trailing gown to be heard.

Kimi felt for Bentley's hand. Without a word they followed Patina on what seemed like an endless walk until eventually the shelves and columns were met by a huge expanse of white brick wall. Arranged in a square around a black coffee table holding two glasses of water, four plush red sofas awaited. Patina sprawled herself across the one next to the wall. She waved them to sit opposite. Which they did.

Golden hair in soft waves, features smooth and pleasant, Patina stared at Kimi for some time. Kimi got the feeling she was being scanned - or something like it. She noted Patina's green eyes and remembered that they had no pupils.

"On the table before you," Patina eventually spoke, then looked in surprise at the bare coffee table. She lifted her gown, coughed, and a misty secretary shot out like a ghost, whizzed over Kimi and Bentley's heads, and came whistling back, plonked a cardboard box on the table, and vanished back under Patina's gown. "Sorry," Patina huffed, patting her skirt. "Tulpa Bentley, please open the box."

Bentley sat forward, pulled the box to him. It seemed heavy, Kimi thought, and big enough to hold a severed head. She'd seen a film once where-

"The box, Tulpa Bentley. Open the box, honey. It won't bite you."

Bentley peeled back the brown tape and tore it slowly away from the box. He took hold of the flaps. He looked over at Patina who was smiling and flicking her fingers at him to hurry up. Bentley opened the box and looked inside. Kimi relaxed a little when he grinned. He put his hand in and pulled out a jar of sweets. At least they looked like sweets. Chocolate balls or something.

"Try one." Patina was still smiling.

Bentley unscrewed the lid and Kimi immediately smelled delicious dark chocolate. Her mouth watered as Bentley popped one into his mouth. He nodded his approval. "Very nice." He took another then handed the jar to Kimi. The taste was divine. Rich, melt-in-the-mouth, and seasoned with something flowery yet spicy.

"Have another," Patina said.

They did. Patina waited until they had both swallowed before continuing. "The very latest in Heart confectionery. 'Doo-doo's' were invented by Barry, the man Kimi kindly donated mojo to." She smiled proudly at Kimi. "You gave him such a spark. Not only did this man regain his mojo, he blossomed, improved, put his talent to good use. He resurrected the dodo, made it better than ever, and even designed and created enhanced farming. Dodo poop is scooped away and the useful nutrients left therein are flavoured with famoose tears and transformed into these deliciously healthy sweets."

"Healthy?" Bentley said. "We've just eaten poop?"

Kimi felt the fudgy poop nudging up her throat. She realised what the water was for, grabbed up a glass and drank it down. So did Bentley.

"Doo-doos," Patina went on, "although no doubt a luxury, are just one example of how Kimi Jo Nichols has brought changes for the good. One must always take positives from negatives. Doing so is the only way forward."

"There's a negative?" Kimi said.

Patina clasped a hand to her chest. "Yes, sweetie. And I am sorry but negatives have to be dealt with." She rested her hands in her lap. "Almost a year ago, premature Balancer Kimi Jo Nichols coerced fellow balancers, and tulpas - and even our chief of fuzz - to take part in a secret mission."

"I had to get my parents back," Kimi said, feeling suddenly nervous.

"That you did," Patina said. "You did what you had to do, which resulted in triumph for your personal goal. However, success for one is often failure for another, and, sadly, in your case it was the death of a respected greylian General. At least, that is what you tell us."

Kimi felt sick.

"What in bafflecakes is that supposed to mean?" Bentley said in a tone that made Patina's eyebrows rise.

"In Kimi's statement," Patina said, "she tells us the General was shot through the stomach with his own weapon, that she was acting in self-defence, and that the doppelganger paradox caused his implosion which resulted in total disintegration. Therefore, no physical evidence remains to verify her account. As you can imagine, with no evidence that General Cohn is alive or dead, and with his brand new Starburst still missing, the greylian authorities are questioning Kimi's side of the story."

"Well they can't have General Cohn's side," Bentley said. "Because he's where he deserves to be. Please believe me, Adept Patina, I heard his thoughts. He wanted Kimi dead. And he'd already killed her parents."

"Oh I believe you, Tulpa Bentley. I also believe Kimi. We must take nothing away from our heroine's bravery. However, it is the greylian judge we must convince!"

"Judge?" Bentley stood up. Patina waved him back down.

Little Hand tingled sharply. Kimi jumped.

"Tomorrow..." Patina locked eyes with Kimi. "Tomorrow, there is to be a trial."

Bentley stood once more. "You cannot be serious!"

Patina waved him back down. "A trial in which our brave heroine must provide evidence to prove her claims."

But there is no evidence, Kimi thought.

"There is no evidence!" Bentley snapped.

"Oh but there is," Patina said. "We just have to retrieve it."

Footsteps sounded from behind Kimi and Bentley, and they both turned to see a tall man, middle-aged, in a dark suit and tie, his hair combed over his head. Kimi thought there was something familiar about him. As he neared the sofas she spotted the monocle over his left eye. She stood up. "Charlie?"

"Adept Babbage?" Bentley also got to his feet.

The man smiled. "Yes, it's me," he said. Kimi rushed to hug him.

***

7
The Thieving Crow

Babbage took a seat, but not before helping himself to a doo-doo. "Yes my friends. It is I, believe it or not."

"But – but – your – erm," Kimi couldn't find the words.

"I am no longer deformed, my gruesome appearance is no more, and I also have my old legs back. Is that what you were trying to say?"

But how? Kimi thought.

"But how?" Bentley said.

"Once upon a time," Babbage said, "I had to fly back in time to save the life of a certain young girl. I knew that I would die doing so. Too many trips for one not so pure as our heroine meant the end for the old lump I had become."

"You've lost me," Bentley said.

Kimi said, "First time around things went wrong, Bentley. My jump upset things, made the black mountain blow up, and people were killed by flying boulders and lava bombs - including me."

"What?"

"Yes. After I died you cut off my head."

Bentley went white, eyes like saucers.

"There were wars, Tulpa Bentley," Patina said. "Wars

that many thousands lived and died through while Mr Babbage here sought gallantly for a solution. Kimi's brain, or at least part of it, was stolen by the greylians so that they could plunder time. Adept Babbage stole it back and used it to travel back through time himself, to save Kimi from the boulder that would crush her. Doing so prevented those wars from ever coming to pass. But now that Middling has been rebuilt and our heroine is back on the scene – the greylians want some answers."

"I see," Bentley said. "So if we don't give them evidence of Cohn's death…?"

"Not just of his death, Tulpa Bentley, but his intent, his plans to rule time."

"And how exactly can we do that?"

Babbage snapped his fingers. The white wall behind Patina began to waver. One of his little boy clowns emerged, floated through the air, and landed gently at the side of Patina's sofa.

"I used to have five clowns, remember?"

"Yes," Kimi said. "I remember."

Bentley said, "Where's the other four?"

Babbage patted his legs. "Right here," he said. "Let me explain. When the future me went back in time, I gave Kimi a message to relay to the old me, that is the new me once Kimi had changed history by dodging that boulder. Which Kimi did."

"The eyes," Kimi said. "Always get the eyes."

"That was the message?" Bentley helped himself to another doo-doo.

"That's right," Babbage said. "And I knew immediately what I meant."

"I always wondered about that," Kimi said.

"When Kimi's father first uncovered the formula for travelling back in time he used paperclips and marbles as experimental subjects. They would deform, break, yet they would still travel. As the formula grew more specific, he moved onto living subjects. I know this because the rascal sent a Bellamy's Aunt to my breakfast plate which promptly turned itself inside out and ruined my beans."

Kimi remembered seeing that very image on the wall of Babbage's lair.

"Yes, we remember that," Bentley said.

"It was at this point I joined Kimi's father, and with further tweaks the formula was ready for a human subject. I forbade your father to travel. If anything was going to go wrong then it made sense that only one of us should be affected. So I jumped. Yet shortcomings in the formula – in other words the vital ingredient of purity – caused a blip in the jump. I was stuck in time. Stuck in a horrible place, and it was almost an hour before the blip corrected and I arrived at the target time."

"What horrible place?" Kimi said.

"Where the clowns live, Kimi. Where they lurk and play and will rip your guts out with gay abandon and laugh their pretty little socks off while they do so."

"You're getting dramatic," Patina said. "We don't want to scare the girl."

"This is fascinating," Bentley said. "What was this place like? I mean, does it really exist?"

"Yes," Babbage said. "Imagine if you would, a huge elastic band, wrapped around our own time and space."

Bentley nodded. "Yes, I get that."

"Travelling from one set time to a previous time is not unlike travelling via twirly. There's a little discomfort, some of that white mist and a fizzing feeling when you break through at your target time. It is that discomfort which I have come to imagine as the elastic band. And when there is a blip you stay caught up in the elastic band until it rights itself. It's like the ghost train you are riding on has broken down and you can jump out and have a look around before it starts up again."

"So it's like a ghost train?" Kimi said.

"It's everyone's worst nightmare," Babbage said. "At least that's how it was for me. I always was afraid of snakes and spiders and the jungle I found myself in was full of them. I came to a house, my childhood home. The door opened and I was pulled inside, safe I thought, from the spiders and the snakes. I could hear them hissing and scuttling at the door and it took me a moment to calm my nerves enough to realise that I was in my bedroom."

"Fascinating," Bentley repeated.

"But the thing I feared most of all lived in my bedroom. The thing that kept me awake at night as a child. The thing that brought me shrieking from sleep."

"What was it?" Kimi said, taking a drink of water.

"Wallpaper."

"Wallpaper?"

"Yes," Babbage said. "My mother thought I would love to have clowns on my walls. Little boy clowns with patches on their jackets, all smiling the same smile, all posed in varying acrobatic positions. They scared me half to death. In my dreams those smiles had fangs and those fangs would tear at my toes and I'd wake up screaming. Blighted me for years."

"So you had this fear all your life?" Bentley said.

"Never mind that," Kimi said. "Tell us what happened next."

"The clowns started peeling themselves from the wall, just like they did in my nightmares, coming at me with fangs bared. I thought immediately of two options, not realising there were actually three. First option was to retreat, go back the way I had come in, but the spiders and snakes were making plenty of noise out there, so I ruled that one out. Option two was the door across the room. If this were my old home it would lead to a landing. Of course I knew that this was not really my home. I was stuck in a blip in the elastic band waiting for time to hurl me out."

"So was it the landing?" Kimi said.

"No. I closed my eyes and screamed some absurd battle-cry and charged those rotten clowns out of my way. I threw myself through the door and pulled it quickly shut behind me. I was not on the landing. I was back in my room, the clowns were back on the wallpaper, the snakes and spiders still hissing and scuttling outside."

"Wow," Kimi said. "So what did you do?"

"The clowns peeled themselves from the wallpaper again, and this time they grew bigger fangs, longer and more lethal looking. I screamed my battle-cry and ran once more for the landing only to find myself back in my room with the clowns peeling from the walls."

"Nightmare," Kimi said.

"Worse," Babbage said. "This went on for some time. I was sweating profusely, panicking, and on the verge of trying the other door, facing up to the spiders and the snakes. They seemed like a better option. But I didn't."

"You zapped the clowns with stunners?" Kimi offered.

"Ah, good thinking, Kimi, but I forgot to mention, your mojo doesn't work in the band, the blip, whatever you want to call it. I was breathless, sweating like a horse, scared out of my wits, and truth be known I thought I might be on the verge of having a heart attack."

"So how did you get out of it?" Bentley said.

"I faced my fear," Babbage said. "Simple as it sounds but I marched right up to those clowns and poked each one of them in the eye. Told them to scarper."

"And they did?"

"They did just that."

"They turned back into wallpaper?"

"No, they sat on my bed, smiling."

"Creepy."

"Not at all. They were full of offers of help. Told me to sit and be patient, so I did, glad of the rest, and before I knew it the blip was over and I was back in the land of the living."

"And the clowns came with you?"

"Yes. I soon learned that I could summon one or more of them at any time. That they would emerge from the wall or floor, attend my whims, and disappear again just as soon as I wished it."

"So what does this all have to do with Kimi?" Bentley asked.

Babbage took out a handkerchief, dabbed his face. Patina lifted her hem and a secretary left and returned with another glass and a fresh jug of water which jangled with ice cubes. She disappeared back into the swishing folds of Patina's garment. "Thank you." Babbage poured, took a long drink, then: "Thanks to Kimi's message from me to me – about the eyes – I knew where I had to look. Those eyes I had poked to conquer my fears were the very eyes I needed. After a little investigation, one of the clowns offered up his secrets."

Don't talk to me about secrets, Kimi thought.

"Please, no more secrets," Bentley muttered.

Babbage smiled. "It turned out that because the clowns were in fact the essence of self, I could use them to repair my broken body."

"Wow!" Kimi said.

"Indeed," said Bentley.

"But that was not all the clowns could do; they could also hold memories. I learned that everything I experienced whilst in the band, all of it, the snakes and spiders, the running from one room to the same room over and over, the clowns peeling from the walls – every last thing that I witnessed through my eyes and heard through my ears was recorded by the clowns."

"How do you mean?" Bentley said.

"The clowns which Adept Babbage encountered while stuck in the blip were merely the product of his own fears, his own mind," Patina said.

"Like a tulpa?" Kimi offered.

"Similar," Patina said. "But in this case it is an energy built from fear and anxiety and all things troublesome."

"What about the spiders and the snakes?" Bentley said.

"I never did confront them," Babbage said. "I imagine they might act in the same way as the clowns if I were to poke them in the eyes, but I never did. The important thing is the clowns and the information they hold. Watch!" He waved a hand and the clown, who had made himself comfortable crosslegged on the floor, sprang to his feet. "Can we have the lights down?" Babbage said to Patina.

Patina raised a hand and the lights dimmed like they do at the cinema. That's when Kimi realised she had never noticed any actual lights in this huge place.

"You know what to do," Babbage said to the clown.

"Wait!" Patina said, and the lights went up again. "Put your fingers in your ears and keep them there until the clown's head has fully opened!"

"Good call," Babbage said.

Its head? thought Kimi.

"Its head?" said Bentley.

"Don't worry, it doesn't bleed," Babbage said. "Fingers in ears please."

Bentley cupped his hands over his ears. Kimi did the same. Patina did not. She raised a hand once more and the light dimmed. Babbage's silhouette nodded to the clown who stood like a black cut-out shape. "You know what to do," he said again.

Kimi could barely make out the features on the clown's face, but could see enough to make her wince when the clown reached up with pointed index fingers and plunged them into its own eyes. Bentley winced too, she felt it twang in her. Babbage said there would be no blood, but she still expected brains might come gushing from the sockets. She held her breath, linked into Bentley. He put a hand on hers and she almost shut her eyes when the clown's hands began to push and pull.

There was a sound like ripping cloth and the clown's head split open with a deafening screech, and from within bloomed a bright white bubble, expanding in the air above its head. The clown went limp, arms dropped to its sides. The bubble swayed on the clown's neck, its white surface broke into a mist then formed into a crystal clear image of a door. It was like watching TV in high-definition. They hear the soft hisses and the scuttling of spiders and the quickened breath of Babbage as his hand appears, reaching for the door, and in he goes, and the door slams and there is a loud and sharp intake of breath as Babbage halts at the clowns on the wallpaper and at that exact moment the clowns begin peeling themselves from the wall and growing fangs and Babbage charges through them and the next door opens and bangs shut and Babbage's breathing is fast and hard as the clowns begin to peel from the walls and the fangs grow whiter and longer and Babbage charges once more.

"That'll do," Patina said, and the light returned. The bubble they had been watching gave a wobble and sucked itself back into the waiting flaps of the clown's head which folded up and sealed itself.

"That was something else," Bentley said. "But what's that got to do with Kimi?"

Babbage dismissed the clown. He waited until it had vanished into the wall then sat forward in his seat. "To put it simply, Kimi must travel one more time, confront her fear, and bring it back to present as evidence at the trial."

Kimi could feel Bentley's mind whirring. After a moment he spoke, "But you said you had a blip – Kimi doesn't do blips."

Babbage nodded. "Which is why her genius father has come up with his cleverest device yet." He looked to Kimi,

"How are you feeling?"

"Scared out of her wits, I should think," Bentley said. "This is crazy."

Kimi shrugged. "I'm okay, I think."

"Of course she's okay. She's a heroine, a brave heroine," Patina said.

Bentley sighed. Kimi could sense his anxiety.

"There is one thing we must know, Kimi," Babbage said. "Childhood fears are the fears most deeply ingrained. We need to know what yours were. Or more importantly *you* need to know, so that overcoming them will be made easier. So, we need you to think back to your childhood. What did you fear the most?"

She still is a child, Kimi heard Bentley think in the faintest whisper.

"Let me think," she said and closed her eyes. Spiders were never cool, not the way they moved on their slinky legs. Snakes she'd always liked. There wasn't much *to* fear really. Apart from the monster that might have lived under her bed at some point in the past. Even now she might hesitate before swinging her legs out of bed and ready herself for the slick wet fingers snatching at her ankles. Kimi's heart was banging. She opened her eyes. "I had a thing under my bed."

"What did it look like?" Babbage asked.

"I – I never saw, only thought – I don't know."

"Think, Kimi, this is important. You must have assigned some image to this imaginary monster."

"Well, yes I suppose. It started with Mum's leather gloves. They were smooth and black and she used to leave them over the arm of the sofa. Gave me the creeps. So I got to imagining them under my bed, waiting to grab at me."

"So your monster was a pair of gloves?"

"Not quite. My imagination ran away with itself. The gloves multiplied and soon there was a man with a hundred hands under my bed. One hundred black gloved hands ready to grab me."

"Did you name this man?"

Bentley huffed. "What, like Colin or something?"

"I called him the Gribbley Grabbley Monster."

"I remember!" Bentley said brightly. "You summoned me a few times for reassurance. Had to sleep under your bed before you would go to sleep. Damned uncomfy."

"So this thing you feared did not really exist," Babbage said.

"Only in Kimi's imagination, sir," Bentley said.

"Then that is ideal." Babbage stood up. "Kimi, I need you to prepare your mind for the mission ahead. Think hard about your fears, not just the monster under your bed, but anything you can think of that gave you the shivers at one time, or anything that makes your heart pound right now."

Kimi thought of Perry. Bentley looked at her.

"Tomorrow morning," Babbage went on, "You will be briefed on the device and how it works an hour before the trial."

"Exactly what is this device?" Bentley said. "Is it dangerous?"

"I'm afraid, Tulpa Bentley, the rules of the court are quite strict." Babbage sat back down. "The device is under heavy guard. No detail can be released until Kimi's scheduled briefing."

"Tomorrow morning?"

"Yes."

"And what do Kimi's parents think about this?"

Good point, thought Kimi. "Can I see Mum and Dad now please?"

Babbage sat back, clasped his hands in his lap. "Not until tomorrow, I'm afraid."

It felt as if everyone present were holding their breath. Silence in a place so huge was a whole lot of noise. Tingles, tiny and focused, buzzed softly through Kimi's left arm, across her shoulder, up her neck, and warmed the smallest throb in her brow. Focus was the key here, and Kimi knew it. The last time she had felt the power of her mojo in such a tight and meaningful way was just before she blew a hole in General Cohn's gut.

Bentley broke the silence. "There'd better be good reason for this!"

Patina tutted. "Tulpa Bentley, sweetheart, I could take offense. Speaking to an adept, in my house, in such a way, is not a nice thing."

"I – I wasn't – didn't mean anything – I – I – well, Kimi is only a –"

Patina raised a hand. Her eyes, now swirling sapphires, locked onto Kimi's once again. "Let me put it simply, Kimi. Your father, your mother, and Adept Babbage have invented the most amazing thing. This device, or machine, call it what you will, is so perfectly tuned from long hours and long days of sweat and tears, so finely-tuned that your absolute safety is guaranteed. We did not want to risk leaving this most excellent invention at risk of, shall we say, interference, and so your father and your mother knew it would be best not to leave its side."

"So Mum and Dad are babysitting a machine?" Kimi said.

"That's right," Babbage said. "With your father and mother guarding it at all times it won't be tampered with and we can guarantee your absolute safety."

The throb in her brow threatened to become a headache. The tingles were becoming too much. Kimi felt a sudden desire to conjure a thousand stunners and shove them up Patina's dress.

Babbage stood up. "Briefing tomorrow morning. Ten o'clock sharp. Until then, Tulpa Bentley, you must encourage your balancer to face her fear. The more she can accept the concept now the easier it will be when she enters the blip."

"Good, good. Everyone is happy," Patina said. She lifted her dress and a stream of golden light rushed out. In seconds they were surrounded by a hundred smiling secretaries in their yellow jumpers, wispy legs swirling beneath their waists. "Girls, see my guests to the door!"

Kimi and Bentley were jumped upon, picked up by giggling secretaries who carried them speeding like a train back through the library and dumped them at the little door in the wall. The door opened and they were pushed into the lobby.

"Fourteen," Kimi said.

Bentley looked at her. "Eh?"

"Shrink!"

"Oh." He shrugged, shuddered, shrank to a pleasant looking fourteen year-old.

"Thanks."

"Welcome."

They walked through the lobby and went outside and Kimi set off walking in the sunshine with a chilled breeze on her face.

"Want to twirly back?" Bentley was at her side.

"No thanks. Need the fresh air."

"So, erm, what do you reckon about your fear? Think you'll be bringing the Grabby Monster back?"

Kimi shuddered. "Gribbley Grabbley Monster," she corrected.

"Right. I mean, if it's all in the mind you can overcome it easily then, eh?"

Kimi stood still. She had spotted a crow. A single crow. It was hopping around on the grass near the steps they would soon be heading down. "Watch me," Kimi said, and she ran.

And ran.

The crow saw her coming, moved itself nearer the steps.

And Kimi kept running, focused on the crow as it reached

the top step and stayed there.

"Kimi!" Bentley was catching up, but her legs were gaining speed, pounding the rocky ground and then onto grass which added a spring to her run as she counted the last five bounding leaps, reached a finger to the air and twirled it, making the air spin around her so that when she felt the first fizzle of breaking atoms she had almost reached the bewildered crow on the top step and she leapt high and forward and vanished in a swirl of crow feathers.

"All yours," she said, reappearing behind Bentley.

Bentley turned, eyes wide, and found himself holding a bald crow. "How in the Bellamy's did you do that?"

"Been practicing," Kimi said.

"Very good," Bentley said. "But can you put them back?"

"Huh?"

Bentley twirled a finger and began turning in a circle, faster and faster until he was spinning on one foot. The crow's feathers were sucked into the vortex surrounding him. When he stopped turning and the wind died down the crow was no longer bald. He threw it to the air and it swooped down over Middling cawing like a baby.

"Wow!" Kimi said. "I haven't got that far in the manual yet."

"Shall we go home?" Bentley held out an arm.

Kimi felt a twinge at the right elbow, followed by another at the left. There was a slight wiggle there as if a maggot was pushing out but she knew it was the bristles growing. She stared at Bentley. "Can you do the oldie please?" Bentley shuddered and expanded and the tanned and lined Bentley held out an arm. Should she tell him about her deformities? What if she did and they called the whole thing off? She wasn't sure at all. What would Dad do? He'd think about it logically and come up with the best possible answer. But best for what? Another twinge at the right heel, followed by the right. "Bentley. There's something I've been meaning to tell you. Something weird."

Bentley, who still had his arm out, put it down by his side. "What kind of weird?"

Kimi let out a great breath. It was now or never. She would roll up a sleeve, show him an elbow, see what reaction it got. "It's this." She took a step closer and Bentley did the same. She took hold of her sleeve. A screeching caw, a rush of black, a squabble of beak, claw, and feathers, a thump in the chest and Kimi was thrown onto her backside. The crow was on her chest, its claws pricking her flesh. It opened its beak, jabbed. Kimi yelped and scrambled and flung her arms at the beast but it was strong and it jabbed again and again at Kimi's neck until she heard her necklace snap and the crow snatched it away and took flight.

She sat up, a little dazed. Bentley was poised, silvery stunners dripping from his clenched hand, watching the crow with the dangling necklace glinting in the sun, lifting higher and higher into the cloudless duck-egg sky. Then it started to rain. Heavy thudding drops that soon became a downpour. Bentley threw the stunners over his shoulder and they bounced around in the falling rain as he took Kimi's hands and pulled her to her feet. He said nothing. Spun his finger and in a twirl they were back at the Rabbit's Foot, standing in the doorway.

The bar area was busy. Big Sue shouted hello. Perry, lifting a barrel of pommy juice onto the bar, paused and winked and flashed his white teeth.

"Stinking, thieving crow," Bentley said. "You okay?"

"It nicked my necklace. I only had it five minutes. Mr Purse will not be happy."

"Yes, that was rather weird." Bentley said. "Are you hurt?"

"No, I'm fine."

"So what was it you wanted to tell me?"

Little Hand suddenly tingled like it was being stung by

wasps. Kimi yelped, pulled Little Hand to her stomach, and bent over double. Bentley caught her, made a fuss. She pushed him away, looked around at the hushed bar. All eyes were on her.

"I've got a headache," she said. "I need to lie down."

"Of course," Bentley said. "I understand. Get some rest. Come down later for the celebrations."

It seemed an odd thing to be celebrating something that had not yet been achieved. But Kimi wasn't going to argue. She raised a finger and twirled herself back to her room.

***

8
The Remorseful Crow

Stella was sitting at the round table in front of the dresser. She'd swapped jeans and leather jacket for Twilight pyjamas and was peering intently at the bliss fly's tongue she was varnishing.

"Do you always varnish in your pee-jays?" Kimi said.

"Always," Stella said. Then: "Do you think Perry would make a good vampire?"

"I'm not into vampires." Kimi sat at the table. Stella's display was looking a bit ropey. The Bellamy's Aunt sagged and bulged and did not look much like the toad it was meant to be.

"I never thought of taking this to Florida. Needs a bit of restoration now." Stella stroked some final touches of varnish onto the bliss fly's probe and the toad's pink tongue into which the probe was probing. "Speaking of Perry, do you -"

"Let's not." Kimi pushed her chair back, went to her bed, and sat on its edge.

Stella put the brush down, placed the glass dome back over the display. "I can sense you're not your usual chirpy self. You didn't like the tour?"

Kimi began to cry. She buried her face in her hands and when she felt Stella's consoling touch upon her shoulders she stood from the bed and twirled herself into the bathroom, where she was greeted by a flourish of newspaper and a manly screech. As the papers settled, Kimi saw Perry staring wide-eyed from the toilet seat with his trousers round his ankles, so she twirled herself backwards through the door and bumped into Big Sue. The tray of goodies he was carrying flew from his hands and clattered the floor.

"Oh my," he said, grabbing Kimi by the scruff to stop her falling down the stairs. "I was bringing you and Stella some refreshments. Is there something wrong, dear?"

Kimi looked up at him. "Sorry. I'll clean it up."

Big Sue shook his big head. "You go on up. You look half-terrified. I'll clean this up and bring some fresh for you. Yes?"

Kimi nodded. "Thank you." She ran up the stairs, darted into the bedroom, flung herself on her bed and let the tears out until she sobbed to a stop. She looked up to see Stella staring at her.

"Now you've got me worried," Stella said. "Please tell me what happened."

"Well, if you really want to know." She took a breath. "I'm on trial tomorrow. I have to time-travel into the blip, tame the Gribbley, bring him back here so he can peel his head open and prove my innocence, *and* I've been attacked by a crow that nicked my new necklace, *and* I've got so many bristles I could brush my hair with my elbow - and on top of all that I've just bumped into Perry on the bog."

Stella snorted.

There was a tap on the door. Big Sue ducked inside with a fresh tray of sandwiches and juice. "Party starts in two hours, girls. Make sure you're ready and presentable." He placed the tray on the table, ruffled Kimi's hair with a big hand, and ducked back out again. The door clicked shut.

"Perry? On the bog? Really?"
Kimi nodded.
Stella burst out laughing.

Once Stella had calmed down enough to listen, Kimi joined her at the table. She recounted the tour, the meeting with Patina and Babbage, the terrible sight of the clown pulling its head apart, and after that the crazy crow attack, but all Stella was interested in was the colour of Perry's underpants.

"Pink, actually," Kimi said.

Stella's eyebrows disappeared into her blonde fringe. "No way!"

"Of course they weren't pink," Kimi said. "I didn't hang around long enough to see."

"I would have," Stella said. She picked up a sandwich and took a great bite. "Get one. They're really nice. Egg and tomato."

Kimi had no appetite. She noticed her pomegranate mood lantern on the dresser, reached for it, placed it on the table. She felt like a wreck. "I'm worried about tomorrow." She tapped the lantern gently on its top. Faint amber light glowed from the carved crows running around its surface.

"I'd be more worried about seeing Perry." Stella wiped her mouth with a napkin.

Kimi placed a hand on the glowing pomegranate and the light went out. "There's no way I'm going to this party. I couldn't look him in the face."

"Why don't we go see what he's up to?"

"Are you mad?"

"He doesn't have to see us."

"Don't tell me - you've got an invisibility cloak?"

Stella leant forward, whispered: "Remember the secret room?"

"Of course. I wonder if it's still there."

"I've been waiting for you to come back so we could find

out."

A visit to the secret room and the amazing scope seemed like a good idea. At least it would take her mind off other things. Kimi picked up her lantern. "Let's do it."

They crept down to the second landing and into the storeroom. Once inside, Kimi tapped her lantern: "Moodirecto." Amber light flowed from the front and lit their way to the bottom shelf containing the heavy drums of Oil of Bull Boil.

Stella removed two of the drums. "The vent's still there." She crawled in and unhooked the panel. Kimi passed her lantern and followed Stella into the narrow space. As before, they came to the flap in the vent wall, lifted it and crawled through and into the second passageway. "Looks promising," Stella whispered as she neared the end. She pushed through the flap then helped Kimi inside.

"Light!" Stella said. The shrivelled pomegranate on the ceiling gave a little `*pffft*` and emitted a pale yellow light. A large spider crawled from the carved opening and clung to its rim. Shadows of its arched legs striped the walls. Stella tapped the lantern off and handed it to Kimi.

The tiny room was as they had left it. There were two narrow stools and a walking stick with a dodo skull and beak for a handle. They placed the stools against the walls and sat facing each other with legs spread and knees almost touching. Stella picked up the walking stick and used the beak to press the knot in the wood floor which made a double click then released and there was a puff of dust as the scope's circular shape appeared and began to rise with the faintest vibration.

Kimi watched Stella's grin disappear behind the black metal of the ascending scope. `Viewport 1` came to rest at Kimi's eyelevel. She unhooked the headphones and placed them on her head. Stella was doing the same.

Kimi's heart leapt into her mouth the second her eyes

met the viewport glass. The image was circular and slightly distorted, and the angle from above did not show much other than hair and shoulders, but it was definitely Perry. The was someone else is the cubicle with him – the girl with the golden hair – the harpist. He was saying something, but Kimi couldn't quite hear what.

"Nothing interesting here," Stella said. "What about you?"

"Perry," Kimi whispered. "He's with that girl with the golden hair."

"Yeah, Gorgeous."

"What?"

"That's her name... Gorgeous."

"What kind of name is that?"

"I like it."

"You would. Where's she from?"

"She lives with Perry."

"I don't like her."

"You haven't even met her. She's nice."

"Not sure I want to. Perry's probably telling her about Kimi Nichols, bathroom intruder extraordinaire."

"Don't be daft."

"I'm serious. I can never face him again."

"You're going to have to. Tonight's gathering is all for you. You can't let people down. Oh, look who I just spied."

Stella spun the scope and `Viewport 6` stopped in front of Kimi. "Who?"

"Take a look!"

Kimi looked. Rehd and Ruthie had walked in. Rehd in his best waistcoat and breeches and Ruthie in a blue satin frock. They had made an effort. Even Rehd's hair appeared freshly-washed and fluffy. They were met by Big Sue who started telling them of the wonderful canapés he'd made.

"Aren't they sweet?" Stella said.

"Sweet, yes," Kimi agreed.

"We should get ready."
"To go down?"
"Yes, to go down."
"Do I have to?"
"Yes, you do."
"Why?"
"Because it's your party."
"Then I have a right to cancel it?"

Stella took up the walking stick, pressed the knot in the floor, and the scope descended, folding in on itself with a click and a drop and a click and a drop. Stella looked sternly at Kimi. "Sorry Cinders, but it is imperative you go to the ball."

"What if I'm ill?"
"Are you?"
"Well…"
"Listen. I've been ordered to see that you turn up safe and well. And as your friend and mentor I'll make sure that happens."
"Ordered?"
"Yes. When you were on your tour I was visited by Charlie."
"Babbage?"
"Aye, Babbage. He said tough times were ahead for our hero, and that you would tell me all about it when you got back. Which you did. He also said it was my responsibility to look after you, and to make sure you attended tonight's little do because he has some special news for you."
"What special news?"
"He didn't say and I knew not to ask. So, who's using the bathroom first?"

*

In the bathroom, with the door bolted and Stella waiting outside, Kimi washed her face, brushed her hair, tied it back, then examined the marks on her nose. They had grown a little more elongated, indented a little deeper. She applied concealer without looking too closely. She rolled up her sleeves, saw the dark bristles, felt a lurch in her stomach and quickly hid them again. She did not bother inspecting her heels. She unbolted the door, smiled at Stella. "Let's get this over with."

Kimi went lightly down the stairs, trying to make as quiet an entrance as possible.

"Ohhhhh, here she is!" Big Sue's big mouth.

Someone started clapping and the applause was infectious. Thirty or forty people, adepts, monkeys, tulpas, and one greylian: Granp. All of them clapped and cheered.

Rehd marched over. Ruthie, on his arm, with a tumbler of pommy juice in hand, fluttered her false eyelashes. "Kimi, I've missed you so much. And you, Stella. Isn't it good to be home." She raised her glass. "Here's to you!"

Kimi bent to kiss Ruthie on the forehead. She thought about hugging Rehd, but he was standing tall in front of the other monkeys. He smiled and nodded.

There was no sign of Babbage. Kimi wondered what news he would bring. She hoped it might be that this trial thing was all a joke and that she could go home to Mousehole for a holiday.

"Ah-ha!" came a raspy voice from behind which grated down Kimi's spine. A fat hand landed on her shoulder and spun her round. Blavatsky. Same green suit bulging at the buttons. Same flaky scalp and wispy hair and eyes like currants in dough. "Good girl," she said with a twisted grin. "You did well, Miss Nichols, for a premature, despite the many rules you broke. Let's hope you do us proud tomorrow, too. Only this time stick to the rules, won't you?" She patted Kimi's shoulder then sniffed at the air. "Something smells wonderful. I haven't had a bite all day." She looked Kimi up and down. "Could do with a decent meal inside you, Miss Nichols. Make sure you power up for tomorrow's mission won't you."

Kimi nodded. "Yes, Miss."

"Very good," Blavatsky said, and wandered into the crowd.

"Shall we mingle or stand here and just meet and greet?" Stella said.

"Best to mingle," Rehd said. "Time goes quicker."

Ruthie nudged him in the ribs. "He wanted to come in his Kong tee," she said. "But I said over my dead simian body, no way no sir."

Rehd humphed.

"Mingling, I suppose," Kimi said. The bar area, the stuffy and airless cubicles, seemed so small with so many bodies to-ing and fro-ing. Stella dragged her around and Kimi shook hand after hand and accepted thanks and good wishes and pats on the back and eventually found herself being pushed into a cubicle seat, Stella jamming herself in beside her, and there was Perry and the golden-haired girl called Gorgeous.

The girl smiled a beautiful smile. Lips as smooth as her silken skin and her silver satin dress. Cheekbones sleek and curved and so delicately pronounced. Her neck long and slender, her eyes the colours of autumn. And when she spoke it was with a soft, enchanting tone. "I'm Gorgeous," she said. She held out a hand as smooth as milk, nails black and perfectly manicured.

Kimi took it, felt a flow of coldness. "Pleased to meet you. I'm Kimi."

The girl smiled, took her hand back and snuggled into Perry.

"Hi girls," Perry said.

Silence. Even over the chatter in the room, Kimi could hear Stella breathing. Perry was smiling. She wasn't looking at him, of course not. She was staring at the ceiling, and could see his bright smile out of the corner of her eye. She felt her face warming, so focused on looking for any clue as to where the scope lens might be hidden.

"Kimi!"

Kimi jumped.

Perry was beckoning her to move closer.

She leant in a little, so did Stella.

"I have something to tell you, but only in private."

Kimi swallowed. "I – I'm sorry about before." The words came out without any prompting.

Perry shook his head. "Forget that. I need to speak to you in private. Your room. As soon as possible. It won't take long."

Kimi could feel Gorgeous's eyes upon her like laser beams on snow.

"Shoot off now," Stella said. "Look…" They all looked to the kitchen door. Big Sue had entered the room balancing two huge platters of canapés on his great palms. "No one will miss you when there's grub to be had."

"Thanks," Kimi said, and before she could argue, Perry had taken her by the hand and led her from the room. He went quickly up the stairs and Kimi followed. She opened the bedroom door and they went in. Kimi did not immediately order the lights on. On the sill outside the window, a crow stood silhouetted against the pale night light. When it saw Kimi the crow tapped on the window. There was something dangling from its beak.

"That looks like my necklace…" Kimi went to the window, readying a bunch of stunners in her right hand.

"Be careful," Perry said.

But she did not have to use them. The crow dropped the necklace and took flight. It screeched something which sounded like `*Sorry*` but Kimi wasn't quite sure. She opened the window, retrieved the necklace, locked the window, then ordered the lights on.

"It's broken," Perry said, examining the snapped chain.

"Horrible thing snatched it from me earlier. It was a present from Mr Purse."

"I have heard of crows stealing shiny things," Perry said. "But never returning them."

"Did you hear it say `sorry`? I'm sure I did."

"Maybe it realised it had stolen from Heart's hero and felt guilty. Let me see." Perry took the necklace, closed a hand around it. His fist lit up with a golden glow, then faded. He opened his hand. "Good as new," he said and fixed the necklace back around Kimi's neck.

"Cool," was all she could say. She wanted to ask Perry what else his mojo could do but the words would not come out. Instead she sat at the table, hoping that he would speak first.

"This room is clean?" Perry sat on her bed.

"Er, what do you mean?"

"No bugs, listening devices, that kind of thing."

Kimi shrugged. "Bentley and Sue have just redecorated. I'm sure they would have found any bugs. Anyway, who'd want to listen to Stella snoring? Not good."

Perry laughed. "Here," he said, and patted the bed.

The room was quiet. Only the hum of chatter from the bar below. Then the harp started up. A faint tinkle. Kimi went over, sat on the bed. There was a metre between them. His hair looked nice. Her heart fluttered at her ribs. "I'm really sorry about before," she said again. "It was an accident, I was a bit upset – I – I hope I didn't spoil your – erm, ruin your – erm."

"Kimi, I said forget that. I have permission from Adept Babbage to give you some news."

"Stella said something about Charlie coming."

"He's not coming. He's in your dad's workshop, checking over the calculations for tomorrow's jump, and he wants no visitors, no interruptions until the briefing in the morning. There's something I thought it best you know. I asked Adept Babbage if I could tell you, and he said as long as I did it in private, and that you agreed to keep it to yourself."

"What is it?"

Perry glanced over his shoulder, then moved closer. "Tomorrow, I'm coming along with you."

"To the blip? How? Why?"

"I'm fearless," Perry said. "Or so the tests have shown. Out of all the volunteers I was the only one who passed every test. Nothing scares me, it seems. Not even apparitions in the bathroom," he grinned.

Despite the fiercely burning cheeks, Kimi said, "So if you come into the blip with me, there would be no fears for you to worry about."

"Correct. Which means I will be there to watch your back."

"That's great," Kimi said. "Really great."

"You must keep this to yourself."

Kimi nodded. "Of course I will."

"There's one other thing – the main reason why I'm going – your dad and Adept Babbage believe that we might bump into another fear inside the blip. The theory is that because you jumped with General Cohn, it is possible that he also left his fear behind."

"But he's dead."

"That doesn't mean his fear will be. It may have vanished when he died. He may have even been fearless. We just don't know. And even if we do meet his fear, it doesn't necessarily mean it will be harmful to us. Anyway, I will be there to safeguard you."

Kimi stared at him. Thoughts of General Cohn, when he attacked her, when he tried to suck her brains out with his revolting tongue, came rushing back. She saw his eyes explode into black mush, saw the metallic floor of the

Starburst through the hole in his gut.

"Kimi, you don't look very happy about this?"

"Oh yes. I'm happy. And grateful. Thank you."

"I wasn't looking for thanks, Kimi. We owe you, and I will make sure you stay safe and come back and prove your innocence. Together we will do that." He smiled. This close she could smell his minty breath.

"Perry…"

"Yes?"

"That girl – Gorgeous. She's very pretty."

"Of course. She's gorgeous."

Questions were queuing up in Kimi's throat in quick succession – *I hear you live together? - Surely you're too young to be married – (I didn't look for a ring – no wait, I'm too young to be looking for rings) - Do you love her? - Does she look THAT gorgeous first thing in a morning?* – but the question that won the battle and rolled right on out was a beauty…

"Will you marry me?"

Simple as that.

Kimi could have shrivelled up and died.

Perry looked as if he hadn't heard her, so she exploded into laughter. Perry laughed too. She tapped his knee and laughed again and thought her cheeks might burst into flames. "I'm such a kidder," she said and felt like the biggest numpty. "Oh come here!" she said and wrapped her arms around him and gave him the tightest hug before bouncing back onto the bed and continuing with the silly giggles.

"Good joke," Perry said. "Funny. Right then, Kimi, we had best get back. I hope you feel better and sleep soundly, knowing that you will have a companion for your mission."

"Oh I do. I really, really do," she panted.

He stood from the bed. "I'll go first. And remember," he tapped his nose, "keep it to yourself!"

"Myself," Kimi said with a smile.

"Okay. See you in a bit."

"In a bit."

Perry left, closed the door quietly.

"Lights," Kimi said and the room dropped into darkness. She put her burning face in her hands, lay back on the bed and thought about candyfloss and carousels and crows with no feathers.

***

9
DRINK ME

In the moon-brushed darkness with the tinkling harp and muffled chatter from downstairs at odds with her thumping pulse, Kimi's thoughts turned to the Gribbley Grabbley Monster. He could be under her bed right now, knobbly fingers poised to grasp a straying foot. Of course there was no monster under the bed. It was years since she last thought of it. Well, probably two years, at least. If it was there, lurking, then only the mattress she was lying on and some wooden slats separated them. A real monster would rip its way through the slats and claw the mattress to shreds, wrap its bony hands around her neck and she would be pulled screaming into monster land.

"Lights!" Kimi sat up, took a deep breath, and had a sudden yet amazing idea. "Come quickly, Bentley," she said to the room, then swung her feet to the floor and went to the window. Across the street the rain-soaked walls of her parents' house glistened in the moonlight. The sound of furious clicking came and went as a shimmering globe flew past the window – the famoose did not stop to chat. "Come on, Bentley," Kimi said again. There was a whoosh and a blast of air. Kimi turned to see Stella. Her eyes were bright, cheeks red, grin wider than a wide-mouthed frog, and there was something green stuck in the gap between her teeth. She was wearing her periwinkle leather jacket, had a plate in one hand and a brown BoZone bag in the other. "Hi," she said, then hiccupped.

"Where's Bentley?" Kimi asked.

Stella put the plate on the table. It held three small, round crackers, each spread with dark green sludge. "Brought you these before they all go. They're terrific, Kimi. Big Sue won't say what's in them, but he calls them his bog specials. Try one!"

"I'm really not hungry thanks. Where's Bentley?"

"He sends his apologies. He's feeling a bit off. Hot flushes and tingling spine. I told him it's because he's getting old. Do you think it's because he's getting old?" She rested the BoZone bag on the table. "LOOK at this!" She dug a hand in and whipped out a pair of leather trousers. Periwinkle to match her jacket. "How cool are these?" Kicking off her jeans whilst giggling, she pulled on the periwinkle trousers and struck a pose. "You like?"

"Give me a twirl," Kimi said, dryly.

Stella obliged, but shouldn't have really because the whoosh of wind came quick and fast and with a blast that blew Kimi's hair around and made her cheeks wobble.

Stella was gone. The thud and clatter on the tiles above sounded like someone had landed on the roof. Which of course they had. Kimi stepped back as dust sprinkled from the rafters. Another gust of wind and Stella was on her backside on the floor.

"Ouch," she said.

"How much pommy juice you had?"

"Only one. Honest. It's these bog crackers. Make you hyper. Try one."

"I'm hyper enough thanks. Listen, I need a favour."

Stella got up off the floor, sat at the table, and grinned, the green sludge still stuck between her teeth. "Yeah?"

Kimi sat across from Stella and looked her in the eye. "I've discovered a new skill," she whispered.

"No way?"

"Yes. I can predict the future."

Stella laughed. "Balancers can't do that. Nobody can really do that."

"It's true. Watch." Kimi closed her eyes, put her fingers and thumbs together and spread her arms wide. She made a low humming sound. She could hear Stella stifling a laugh but kept on humming. She swayed a little from side to side and decided to add to the effect with a little stretch. She focused on her waist and felt the flesh and muscle loosen as her upper body began to rise and the skin and bone altered its substance to that of elastic, and she swayed some more and even gave a little moan before sucking back down to her normal shape and size. She snapped her eyes open and stared menacingly at Stella.

"You're mad," Stella said.

"I've seen the future," Kimi said, trying her hardest to be serious.

Stella picked up two of the bog crackers, pressed them together and popped them in her mouth. "Let me guess… I'm gonna get fat?"

Kimi shook her head solemnly from side to side. "Worse than that. So much worse than that."

Stella swallowed the crackers. "You're freaking me out. Come join the party before you miss it."

"That's just it," Kimi said. "You can't go back down. You mustn't, Stella. Oh Stella."

"Stop it, Kimi. You're not funny."

"No, but YOU will be!"

"What do you mean?" Stella said. The green sludge between her teeth waggled as she spoke.

"When you go downstairs, people will laugh at you,

talk about you behind your back, snigger and point and whisper."

"I'm going." Stella stood up.

"But wait! The future can be altered," Kimi said.

"And exactly *why* would they laugh at me?"

"I can make it so they don't," Kimi said.

"I don't like where this is going," Stella said. "Are you feeling all right? You don't look all right. And what did you want Bentley for anyway?"

Kimi sighed. "I – I don't want to go back down. I – I'm tired, and I just-"

Stella narrowed her eyes. "What did Perry want?"

"I – I can't tell you. Sorry."

"Secrets?"

"Sorry."

"Did you kiss?"

"Of course not."

Stella sat back down. "What's going on, Kimi?"

Kimi sighed. "I'm going home."

"How so?"

"Tonight. I was going to tell Bentley that I felt unwell, headache or something, and ask him to thank everyone and that I'd see him in the morning."

"And then you were going home?"

"Yes."

"To Mousehole?"

"Yes."

"Even though your old place has been locked up for almost a year."

"Yes."

"Even though your dad confirmed they'd found residue from at least twenty greylian visits."

"Er, yes."

"Even though there's UFO sightings every week within a five mile radius of your bedroom."

"Er..."

"Even though all the cats and dogs on your street have gone missing and we all know what bounty hunters do to cats and dogs."

Kimi did not answer.

"You're not going home."

"You can't really stop me."

Stella was quick. "I could rat on you to everyone, I could grab you right now and twirl you to the fuzz house, I could summon Sue and tie you to his leg, or I could just plain old punch you on the nose and knock some sense into you."

Kimi had not noticed the stunner being formed, and didn't really see it until it was inches from her nose. It struck with a spongy shudder and her head was lolling on her neck. She gripped the table and closed her eyes to steady herself and when she was once again coherent and the feeling of being a vibrating gong had passed, she found she was tied to her chair with thick ropes of green mist, which were still reeling from Stella's fingertips and coiling downwards round her legs.

"Unless you tell me what's going on, you're staying there until morning," Stella said.

"I thought you were my friend."

"I am. That's why I'm not letting you do something totally stupid. Greylian bounty hunters are watching your old place. You'd be abducted the second you show up. Besides, you've never twirled dimensionally before – and that's a danger in itself."

"I only want a quick look. Please."

Stella shook her head. "Look at the facts, Kimi. First you disappear up here with Perry – God knows what you were doing – then you go all gaga and turn into madame Zaza, clairvoyant. And now you want to jump into a greylian bounty hunter's arms – because that's what you'd be doing – assuming you were successful at dimensional twirling, of course."

"What's so hard about it?"

"As if I'd tell you."

Kimi sighed. "I need to get away."

"From what?"

"All of it. The trial, the confronting my fear thing… and…"

"And?"

Silence.

"Those bristle things," Stella said. "Have they got worse?"

"A little," Kimi said. "I can feel them there all the time."

"Maybe we should tell Bentley?"

Kimi had already tried that but each time she went to speak to him she was interrupted by someone – or some*thing*. "I – I've decided to tell him after the trial."

"If you tell him now they might put the trial off."

Kimi thought about that but it didn't seem right. Dad always said it was better not to put things off because they always got worse when you put them off. "No, I'd rather get it over with."

"Will you come back down to the party?"

"I – I can't."

"What do you mean you can't?"

Silence.

"There's something you're not telling me, Kimi. We'll sit here all night if we have to."

Kimi sighed. "Untie me and I'll tell you."

Stella leant her elbows on the table, extended her fingers and reeled the green mist back into herself. "Okay – tell me."

"I really embarrassed myself in front of Perry."

"Oh wow!" Stella brightened, sat up, and really did look like a rabbit with the green stuff hanging from her teeth. "You kissed him didn't you?"

"Worse than that."

"Worse? Like you sang or something?"

"Funny. No."

"You farted didn't you? Don't tell me you let one go in front of him?"

"I wish," Kimi said.

"What then?"

"I – I only went and…"

"Went and what?"

"I asked him to…"

Stella's eyes were drooling. "What, what?"

"I asked him to marry me."

Stella seemed to have turned to stone. But only for two seconds before she was making excited wheezing sounds and whacking the table with a palm.

"It's not at all funny," Kimi said. "I don't even know why I said it. It just came out."

Stella was crying now. Real tears and belly-laughs.

Kimi got up and went to her bed, sat on it, waited for Stella to calm down. "I know I'm stupid, but can you see why I can't go down there?"

"Ach, Kimi," Stella wiped her eyes. "I haven't hooted like that since I caught Big Sue skinny-dipping in the pond at midnight. Did you really ask him to marry you?"

"Well, the memory of it is a blur, but I'm sure I said it."

"What did he say?"

"He laughed."

"Oh crap."

"Exactly."

"What did Perry want anyway?"

Kimi thought for a second. "I've been sworn to secrecy. However, if you tell me why it's so hard to twirl through dimensions, I'll tell you what Perry wanted."

"You can't go home, Kimi. You would be captured within minutes."

"I know, I understand that now. I guess I was just running away. I do miss the place."

"It's extra focus. That's all. Projecting the focus visually – and visually *is* the key for successful dimensional twirling."

"What do you mean by 'visually'?"

"Imagine your focus coming out of your head and aiming exactly at your target. Imagine it travelling there, imagine it – imagine *you* – landing skilfully at your destination on something tiny like a penny, imagine your focus hitting that spot and think no other thoughts while you're doing it. Fail to project well enough and you can land in trouble."

"What kind of trouble?"

"Examples in the manual show one old woman half-embedded into a pavement. Another man twirled directly inside an elephant in London Zoo. And the remains of one young balancer were apparently found on Mars by one of NASA's probes. No kidding."

"I see," Kimi said. "I'm glad I didn't try it."

"Now tell me."

"What?"

"What Perry wanted."

"Oh."

"Oh?"

"Well, I didn't think you'd tell me how to twirl."

"Ach, I told you because it's in the manual anyway. And it wouldn't take much thinking on your part to work that one out. And you need to know how dangerous it is. Get your focus wrong and the greylians would be abducting a dead body."

"Okay," Kimi said. "Promise you won't let on to anyone that you know?"

Stella nodded. "You know you can trust me."

"Well, he sat on my bed, and he said…"

"And where were you at this point?"

"He asked me to join him."

"On the bed?"
"Yeah."
"So you did?"
"Yeah, I sat on the bed."
"What'd he say?"

Kimi explained that it was no biggie. That Perry had revealed his part in the mission, that he was fearless, and that General Cohn's fear might need dealing with.

"And then you asked him to marry you?"

Kimi nodded. "Crap a numpty, Stella. I'm a total idiot. And I just know he'll have told his girlfriend. I can't ever go downstairs again."

"What girlfriend?"
"That sickly pale gorgeous what's-her-face."
"Gorgeous? The harpist?"
"Yes, her."

"That's not Perry's girlfriend. That's his tulpa, Gorgeous the Ghost. She's a cool dude really."

"His tulpa?" Kimi put her head in her hands.

"Easy mistake to make though. She is a bit touchy feely. Gives me the creeps sometimes."

"I wish I was dead."

Stella came over, hugged her. "Listen, I understand why you don't want to back to the party. I'll go down and make some excuses. Give me half an hour and I'll fetch us some hot chocolate, okay?"

"I'd like that."

Stella made for the door.

"Stella!"
"Yeah?"
"Thanks."

Stella winked. "See you in a bit." And the door closed behind her.

Kimi picked up her mood lantern, stashed it in her jacket pocket, stood in the centre of the room, imagined a dark horn of pure focus projecting from her brow, growing slowly outwards like Pinocchio's nose, its destination the sandy cove of Mousehole harbour where, even if things went wrong, she would only end up stuck in sand. She closed her eyes, thought of home, the beach, the sand, and focused hard before raising a hand and twirling the air.

The whoosh was cold and chilling to the bone, the fizzling holes painstakingly stretched, the irritating white noise felt like pins in the skull, the transfer of atoms through space and dimension an hallucination of focused dreams and beating wings and Moonface, Moonface shouting DRINK ME, DRINK ME. But above all this was something new, something stifling. She was choking, drinking down harsh salty water.

***

10
There's no place like home

Suffocating, struggling against a great weight, before a feeling of rising through the grey murk, rising towards a pale circle of light. And suddenly she was free, breaking the surface, thrashing and retching wildly. The light had been the moon and she bobbed there beneath it and stared at Mousehole harbour. It was raining.

The harbour and Kimi's street beyond were deserted. Not a person to be seen. Rows of small boats were parked on the sand – the sand she should have landed on. The houses that ran the curve of the harbour were all in darkness, including her own right in the middle which looked homely and inviting despite its vacant appearance. She moved softly towards the shore, teeth chattering from the ice-cold water, not taking her eyes off her bedroom window. Her feet touched pebbles. She waded from the water, all the time watching her home and the darkness above it as the moon slipped behind the cloud.

Shivering, and not knowing what her next move could possibly be, she stared at the black panes of her bedroom window. She longed to lie on her bed. Longed to touch every last skull in her collection. She took one step forward, then another, and another, expecting a hand on the shoulder at any second or a greylian abduction beam to snap on and in a blink she would find herself on the other side of the universe. She crept slowly and quietly over the pebbles onto sand where the small boats lay in a line for the night. Quicker now, to the harbour wall where the shadow was black and made her feel just a little bit better. Watching her house and the heavy cloud above it, and shivering uncontrollably, Kimi knew she had to do something, get somewhere warm and dry. But where? She hadn't seen Julie Finbow for a year. For all Julie knew she could be dead. Besides, turning up at Julie's place would put her and her family in danger. And she couldn't do that. There was no way she was going to Aunt Lizzie's either, she would fill her with chickpeas then turn her in.

She had to think of more options. What would Dad do? She didn't know the answer to that because he would tell her she shouldn't have bloody came in the first place. And he would be right. She considered a new option. She could twirl straight back to Heart. She tried to calculate how long she had been here; almost drowning, paddling in, moving slowly, ever so slowly. It might have been five minutes, could even be seven. That would mean five hours at least in Heart time and she would get a rocket up her backside when she got back. She moved along the shadow of the harbour wall and reached the steps. The lamppost on the path above cast a white glow on the steps. If she moved from shadow to light – would she be seen? What to do? What now for the great heroine Kimi Stupid-arse Nichols?

Cold seeped through her, threatened to numb all feeling from her legs. She had to make a move. She could twirl from here to her bedroom. She would put no lights on, be guided by the moonlight through the window. The twirl would dry her, maybe warm her a little. The only other choice was to return to Heart but she did not think she had the strength to get the twirl right. She could end up anywhere, and probably dead. There was only one thing for it. She stared at her bedroom window, raised a trembling hand and began to turn the air. The sand by her feet started to rise in a stuttering swirl. "Come on, come on." Sluggishly but reassuringly the vortex was taking shape, and from the burning numbness of her toes the fizzling began. Kimi closed her eyes, wished for success, and could hear her own heart beating as she passed through the whiteness. The white dimmed to grey and then darkness as her weight returned.

She was dry, no longer shivering, and standing by her bed. The light from the lamppost outside made the shadows soft. Her shelves were bare. Of course, everything had been packed away. But her bed was still there. She climbed carefully onto it, then lay down to keep away from the window. In this semi-darkness she felt safe. She didn't get inside the covers, she just pulled the duvet over herself and snuggled into the pillow. She dared not move, not yet. She was warm and dry now, that's what mattered. But how long until before she was spotted by the greylians? How long until they sent a search-party from Heart? That was actually a good point. She must have been here ten minutes now, which meant ten hours had passed on Heart and they hadn't even come looking. A pang of hunger came from nowhere. She hadn't eaten all day, wondered what food would be in the kitchen, probably Marmite - but no bread. There could be tins in the cupboard, soup and stuff, but that would be out of date. Then she remembered Mum's chocolate stash. Mum always had a pile of stuff on her bedside table. No, that would have been shifted long since. The pang had gone now anyway, the warmth of the duvet was a more soothing distraction. Sleep was inviting, beckoning its promise of safety and security. Kimi closed her eyes and nuzzled the duvet. Warmer now, she decided to sleep and wait for Bentley to come looking. They could do what they wanted with her after that. Just so long as she could have a few warm minutes of peace and quiet. She breathed in the faint smell of fabric conditioner from the duvet cover and thought about clothes on the line and sunshine and the park and playing on the swings with Julie and Julie's laughter as they went higher and higher and-

A scraping sound brought her eyes open. She pulled the cover from her ears and listened hard. There it was again, and it was close, in the room. She tried not to breathe, waited. She felt in her pocket for her lantern, grasped it. If someone was in the room she could at least snap the lantern on in an instant. She thought she heard the sound again, a slight scuffling, and it was coming from - under the bed. Little Hand gave a sharp, momentary buzz.

She listened for the breathing of an intruder. Nothing. Not a sound. Had she imagined it? She was dozing into sleep and imagining things, that's all. Just the mind playing tricks. She lay there, breathing quietly, eyes wide, watching the shadows. Yes, only her mind playing tricks. She should rest and get warm and wait to be rescued by Bentley and make the most of the peace and quiet. Then she remembered that Stella had said Bentley was lying down, feeling unwell; he may not have the strength to get here. That would be all right though because he would send Sue or Stella, or even Rehd. She would be safe soon, she was sure about that. She wished for Bentley to get well soon and sleep beckoned once more. As her eyes were closing she heard it again. A scrape of something, as if someone –or some*thing* was moving on the carpet beneath the bed. Then it stopped.

This was ridiculous. She had heard these noises before, years ago when her imagination brought her the Gribbley with his many knobbled hands encased in black leather gloves that might clasp around her ankles as she got out of bed. She closed her eyes and pulled the duvet over her ears and passed the time counting dodos jumping a fence, but only got to number thirty-seven when she heard a new sound.

A short but definite *hisssss*.

She pulled the duvet from her head, eyes wide in the shadows, and listened. She could hear nothing but her heart - and it was beating too fast. She had an idea. With the stealth of the greatest hunter, lantern in hand, she rolled over slowly to where the bed met the wall. There was just enough gap for the pomegranate lantern to be lowered beneath the bedframe, and once there she would ignite it. True, the Gribbley's leather-gloved hand might just grab hers, but that was better than stepping out of bed and having it grab her ankles. This was a chance she was prepared to take. And if she was quick, whatever was under there would not have time to react. She would lower the lantern to the floor, tap it, and if there was anything under the bed it would cast a shadow into the room. She held the lantern by its crimped top and carefully lowered it through the gap between the bed and the wall, the hairs on her arm prickling as her hand entered the free space beneath the bed frame. Once in place she stretched herself up a little, faced the room so that she could see the carpet and gave the lantern a gentle tap.

Amber light fanned out across the carpet and lit up the base of her rocking chair. Kimi could not believe what she was seeing. Something was casting a shadow, a lumpy shadow, about the size of a large sleeping dog. She tapped the lantern off and pulled her hand away. The room returned to semi-darkness. She waited, listened for any sound. Nothing. She reached through the gap, tapped the lantern again, pulled her hand away. The sleeping-dog shadow on the carpet returned. A lump of a shadow. She studied its outline, looking for any movement. There was none. She thought it might be a pile of old clothes or something that had got shoved under the bed when they were packing stuff away. She reached back through the gap, tapped the lantern off and brought it out.

There was only one thing to do – investigate.

She moved carefully across the bed and readied her left leg before bringing her foot slowly to the carpet. She waited for grasping fingers but none came. She silently swung her right leg from the bed until it touched the floor then slowly pushed herself to her feet. Trembling a little, she took two short steps, turned in silence to face the bed, and waited. Not a sound. She sank carefully to her haunches and let her knees touch the floor.

She lowered her head until her chin was only inches from the carpet. She aimed the lantern at the darkness beneath the bed, and listened. A small but steady tingle made itself known in Little Hand; mojo, detecting someone, some *thing*, some *danger*. It was now or never. She counted down in her head: *five – four –* readying herself for the grasping hands of the Gribbley – *three – two –* she tapped the lantern and the illuminated sight that greeted her brought a flash of hot terror.

The greylian was curled up asleep. Its slit mouth was partly open, revealing the tip of its tongue. It moved slightly causing the scraping sound Kimi had heard earlier. Now seemed like a good time to run for her life, but when the greylian gave a little sleepy hiss, Kimi startled and yelped and the thing's eyes opened sharply. Glossy black ovals stared at her. It smiled the cupcake smile before erupting from its hiding place in a screeching frenzy.

The next few seconds were a blur as Kimi swept up the lantern and fell backwards, twirling the air at the same time. As the vortex intensified, and just before she fell into the wind, the familiar abduction light snapped on, lighting the room and the hissing greylian grasping for her throat in an eerie blue glow. With a blast of orange mojo that exploded from Little Hand without any thought from Kimi, the greylian flew backwards, squealing like pig, and landed on her bed where Kimi watched it writhe in apparent agony before the atoms of her eyes disassembled her to safety.

When the fizzling stopped she was knee-deep in water and facing the black hole that was Mousehole cave. She twirled quickly inside to the damp darkness of the place she used to visit as a kid. Now she was dry and she quickly lit the lantern and followed its beam to the familiar passageway that she knew so well and slipped behind the rock that formed a doorway and into the small enclosure behind. She tapped the lantern off and panted in the darkness of this confined space. The sea lapped at the cave entrance.

She guessed her memories must have brought her to this safe place, or at least close enough to it. Practicing twirly accuracy was a must from now on. She sat on the damp floor and waited for her breathing to settle before edging close to the gap she had slipped through until she could see the opening to the cave and the sea beyond. She expected greylian light beams to be searching to and fro, but there were none. She brought out her lantern and tapped it on and looked around. The cave was small, just as she remembered it. Trails of old seaweed lay about. Apart from that the place was bare and damp, but still she felt safe here. She was about to tap the lantern off when she spotted a ledge she had never noticed before. It was directly across from where she was, at head height, and looked inviting enough to climb up onto and to hide while she figured out what to do next. She went to the ledge, placed the lantern on it, and pulled herself up. Once there she found the ledge to be a perfect fit where she could snuggle into shadows and be safer than down on the cave floor. But she did not stay there. Where the ledge met the rock wall, hidden from view when below it, was a narrow gap. She lowered her cheek to the stone ledge and shone the lantern through the gap. It seemed to show another room beyond, a part of the cave where she would certainly be safer. She lay on her back and slid carefully through the narrow opening and stared in amazement at a chamber she had never seen before. It was big, with crystal stalactites growing down from the ceiling, some of them touching the pool of clear water below in which swam a great many silvery fish flitting and flicking and rolling on the surface. When they rolled the amber glow from the lantern made sparkling patterns on the cavern walls and the gentle ripples of the water were soothing and brought Kimi to sit before the pool's edge where she smiled at the fish and decided that she could rest and sleep awhile. Even the air seemed warmer in here, and she could no longer hear the sea lapping outside, only the silver fish flicking and rolling and rippling the water so peacefully. She rested her head on a convenient rock that was worn down and indented like a pillow. The fish danced and Kimi smiled at them, eyelids closing, opening, closing until the warmth of sleep began to soak into her.

Gentle splashing, like kids kicking puddles. Gentle splashing like – like an oar?

One eye opened. Her vision was hazy but Kimi could see he was real.

"It's all right," the man smiled. "I'm here to intervene."

Kimi sat up, shuffled back away from the pool. "Intervene?"

The man was sitting in a little round wicker boat. He had one hand on a single oar. He wore a knitted jumper with snowflakes and deer on it. He had a bushy white beard and a round face and a navy cap was angled on his head with a silver mermaid badge pinned to its peak.

"You like the fish?" he said.

Kimi nodded. She looked behind him but could not see how he got in.

"You won't tell anyone you've seen me, will you?"

"I won't tell," Kimi said. She remembered the myth about the hermit who lived in the cave and thought this might be him.

"Thank you," the man smiled. "Some things are best kept to yourself, don't you think?"

"Yes, yes I do."

"You aren't saying that just to please me?"

"No, I promise I won't tell."

"One thousand seven hundred and thirteen!"

"Pardon?"

"That's how many fish are in the pool."

"Right."

"I see your nose is coming along well."

"My nose?"

"One thousand, seven hundred and twelve now." He peered sadly at the water. "One just died."

"Oh, sorry," Kimi said, thinking either he was mad or she was dreaming.

"No matter," the man said. "Happens to us all."

"I suppose," Kimi said.

"And I'm not mad. Although that depends on whose definition you believe."

"Pardon?"

"Never mind. Do you have any questions apart from that one?" the man asked.

"What one?"

"The one you just asked."

"I – I didn't."

"Actually you've asked two."

"Two?"

"That's three," the man chuckled.

Kimi shook her head. "This could go on forever."

"Three is a good score," the man said. "Some people go really high."

Kimi nodded.

"The record is held by a man. Five hundred and fifty-seven he got."

"That's not good."

"No it isn't. He was a multiple offender, too."

"Offender?"

"That's four," the man laughed.

Kimi sighed.

"Had to bail him out on a few occasions. He was Prime Minister as well."

There was a frenzy of splashing as the silver fish suddenly went crazy, making the water bubble. Kimi shuffled back a bit. The man in the boat seemed to remember where he was.

"Forgive the digression!" he said loudly to the fish and the fish settled.

"Is this real?" Kimi said without thinking.

The man looked at her.

"That's five, I know," Kimi said.

The man chuckled again. "Do you think this is real?"

She thought of stunballs and felt them forming tingles on her fingertips then let the thought go. She breathed lightly, felt the flutter of loose Elastoplast. She bit her lip until it hurt. "Yes, yes I do," she said.

"Well that's good," the man said. "Because it pains me to be here, Kimi. Really pains me."

He knew her name. That could only mean bad.

"One thousand, seven hundred and ten. Another two gone." The man sighed. "Let's get on with it before the walls cave in."

Kimi swallowed. "Get on with what?"

"Chocolate of course." He grinned and licked his lips and gave a cheeky wink and bobbed in his little boat.

"Chocolate?"

"Chocolate!" He splashed the water with the oar.

"Chocolate?"

"Chocolate – hot chocolate. The most delicious creamy hot chocolate to warm you up."

Kimi was shaking. Her whole body was shaking.

"And a nice dodo sandwich. You haven't eaten all day, you know."

Shaking, shaking, shaking awake.

"Dig in, it's yummy," Stella said.

Kimi stared at Stella in total disbelief.

"You okay, sister?"

"Just a weird dream," Kimi said. "It seemed so real."

"What was it about?"

The memory of almost drowning, of the greylian's hungry eyes and grasping fingers, of the cave and the silvery fish, of the man in the boat with the kind smile, all felt so real. "Just a mixed-up nightmare I guess. How long was I gone? Asleep, I mean."

Stella shrugged. "About an hour. Everyone's gone home, Bentley's feeling a bit better, Big Sue's cleaning up, and Perry didn't mention a thing about your daft proposal."

"Well, good," Kimi said and snatched up a sandwich, took a great bite, swallowed it in two chews, and washed it down with a huge gulp of hot chocolate.

"Oink!" Stella said. "And thanks very much."

"For?" Kimi burped.

"For letting me parade around with Big Sue's bog-sludge hanging from my teeth."

"Oh, sorry," Kimi said. "I should have told you."

"Yes you should. I only had gorgeous Gorgeous pull me to one side and politely tell me my supper was on display."

"Oh no."

"Oh yes. She even tried to pick it out."

"Ewww…"

"Ewww doesn't even begin to cover it. I told her to keep her ghostly paws to herself."

"I don't like her."

"Just because she paws your boyfriend."

"Stop that. Please."

"Fair enough. Oh, and by the by I only put three in your

hot chocolate."

"Three?"

"Laxatives. Revenge for letting me go downstairs like Jenny Green-teeth."

"You haven't?"

"Have so. Should I tell Perry to stay away from the bathroom for the next few hours?"

"You rotten cow."

"You started it. Anyway, what are these fish you've been killing?"

Kimi almost dropped her sandwich. "Fish?"

"In your sleep, you were mumbling that you were killing fish."

"I – I don't know," Kimi said.

"So now you're a fish killer. Nice."

Stella changed into her pyjamas and climbed into bed.

"Did you really put laxatives in my chocolate?"

"Course I didn't you numpty."

Kimi sighed.

"Are you – you know - okay?" Stella asked, pulling the covers up to her neck.

"I think so," Kimi said.

"About tomorrow, the trial."

"I'm scared, Stella."

"Listen Kimi," Stella said. "I'll be here with you all night, and I'll be with you at the trial, and I'll be bringing you home again after it's over. You'll be fine."

"But what if I can't face my fear – what if I can't?"

"Course you can. You can do that easily, Kimi. I know you."

"What if it goes wrong? What if I can't prove I'm innocent, what happens then? No one has mentioned what will happen if I'm found guilty. Will I go to prison?"

"Greylians don't believe in prisons."

"They don't?"

"Waste of resources. They eat the guilty instead."

"You're kidding, right?"

"No I'm not. Kimi, look at the facts. Your dad and Charlie know what they're doing. You've also got your beloved Perry for company. What can go wrong?"

"Please don't call him that. I'm never going to live that down, am I?"

"Well crap a fiancé," Stella said. "You got that right."

"I'll apologise when I see him. Tell him I was under-"

"Stress, yes, we know. Listen, try and get a good sleep, and remember you have the best team behind you. We'll get through it, Kimi. Be a doddle. You'll see."

"A doddle?"

"Abso-crapping-lutely! You trust me?"

"Course I do."

"Good. If you can't sleep, give me a nudge and we'll go for a jog or something."

Kimi smiled. "Okay."

"Night."

"Night, Stella."

"Sweet dreams."

"You too."

"And if they bite…"

"I know – bite them back."

Stella was snoring in less than a minute.

Kimi finished her hot chocolate, set the room to darkness and changed into her pyjamas. She slid under the covers but could not help seeing the image of the greylian under her bed, eyes snapping open, black and hungry eyes. It had all seemed so real. Stella was right, she was stressed to the max. She focused her thoughts on the man in the boat and his warm smile and took the dream for what it was – a comfort – why, the man's smile warmed her just thinking about it. She counted silvery fish flitting and flicking around the boat and rolling the surface with small splashes like an oar turning the water and slipped into a warm encompassing sleep free of any nightmares.

***

11
The Briefing

Kimi woke to bright sunlight streaming through the window from a duck-egg blue sky in which the birds were singing.

"Brought you tea, toast and Marmite," Stella said, shrugging on her jacket.

"Where you going?"

"Sue wants a hand. We're blocking off the street to keep the crowds away."

"Oh." A rock landed in Kimi's stomach.

"Did you kill any more fish?"

"I don't think so," Kimi said. "How long until the briefing?"

"About an hour. How you feeling?"

"Okay, I guess."

"Good. Eat up, get ready, and I'll meet you downstairs." Stella raised a finger, started to twirl, then stopped. "One last thing," she nodded to the floor. "You'd better clean that mess up before Sue sees it." She twirled herself from the room.

Kimi looked over the side of the bed. On the floorboards next to the rug where she had kicked off her trainers before getting into bed was an impossible trail of sand. Kimi stared at the glistening particles, remembered the boatman's kind face. She swept her legs to the side of the bed, intent on jumping out and investigating further, but something snagged in the covers down by her feet and there was a harsh tearing sound. She peeled back the top cover and then the sheet beneath to find huge black spurs growing from her heels. Scaled and glossy, the barbed ends had caught and ripped the sheet. With a surprisingly steady hand, Kimi picked the sheet from each spur and freed her legs.

She did not have to roll up her pyjama sleeves to check her elbows. The bristles, or whatever they were, had multiplied and grown so much they packed out her sleeves. She touched a finger gently to the side of her nose and felt for the indent. It was now a small crater, and so was the one on the other side of her nose. She knew what she had to do. She gathered up her clothes and trainers, brushed the sand into the cracks between the boards, then hoped against all hope that no one was using the bathroom and twirled there in an instant. It was empty. She locked the door and set to work.

Each spur protruding from her heel was a good eight inches long and as thick as a dog's tail. She knew she could not cut them off. They felt like a living part of her. She knew also that the bristles jutting from her elbows were also a part of her. Somehow this was important. Using all four rolls of bandage from the wall cabinet, she carefully strapped the spurs to her legs, flattened them as tightly as possible so that they would not show through her jeans, then did the same with the bristles jutting from her elbows which made a sound like straws being jostled together as she wrapped the bandage around them. Satisfied that the bandages would hold everything in place until the trial was over, it was time to inspect her nose.

The face in the mirror looked different from normal. Her cheekbones appeared more pronounced and formed perfect curves. Her chin and neck looked strong, unbreakable. Her eyes appeared focused and determined.

She brushed her hair roughly and quickly, tied it back, ran the cold tap and washed her face and took some swallows of water. She towelled her face dry and leant in close to the mirror. The craters either side of her nose were big enough for the end of her index finger to rest inside. When she did this, the skin felt thinner, pliable, as if the bone and cartilage behind had vanished. She took a cotton bud and carefully touched the cotton tip to the base of the first crater. The skin gave a little. Kimi felt the urge to apply more pressure. She did so, gently, feeling only a little resistance until the skin broke with a slight puff of air. She moved to the second crater, applied pressure once more until the skin broke. These were like the nostril holes she had seen so many times in her collection of animal skulls, and many times on the heads of the dodos. Kimi was convinced she was turning into a creature of some kind, and if you added in the black spurs at her heels and the bunches of quills bandaged to her arms it seemed most likely that she was turning into a crow.

She moved as close to the mirror as was possible to keep the holes in focus. The skin had torn where the bud had broken it but there was no blood, and no pain. Beyond the broken skin she could see blackness. She took the cotton bud once more and wondered what would happen if she pushed it inside one of the holes. She hesitated, but only for a second or two. Something felt right about this. She steadied her hand and slowly guided the cotton bud into the first hole. She could feel no contact and kept on going until the white cotton tip had vanished inside her face. Nothing. She pulled the bud out, tried the other hole, and watched the white tip vanish inside. She breathed in, felt a rush of air, felt strengthened by it. Felt good about it. Felt this was important, but knew she would have to hide it for now. There was no way she could walk downstairs, or even into a courtroom for that matter with two bloody great holes in her face. The solution was creative but simple. Using the small scissors she'd used to cut the bandages, she shaped two small ovals of Elastoplast, positioned them over the holes in her nose, then used foundation and concealer to do what she thought was a reasonable job of hiding them. She put on a baggy sweat top to cover the padding around her arms, pulled on her jeans, and finally Stella's old red leather jacket - the one with no arms – which was just as well. She gave herself one last look in the mirror. The reflection made a wry smile.

*

The twirl downstairs proved a distracting success. As the wind eased she bowed to the eyes she knew would be looking. The bow showed confidence, brought applause, a pat on the back from Rehd, and a squeeze of the shoulder from Bentley who was looking a lot better in the form of a plausibly nice teen. When Kimi asked him to be his old self because she wanted to feel reassured by the presence of his wisdom during the briefing, Bentley beamed proudly, blossomed into old age and strutted with importance. Stella linked arms with him for the walk across the deserted street while Big Sue waved them away with a tear-stained tea-towel and a sniffling Ruthie clinging to his side.

The painting of her great-great grandfather running up the left side of the front of the house, arm outstretched, shooting flames above the second floor windows, had faded with the years. The advert for pommy juice on the front door looked to have been recently touched up. Kimi took the old key from her pocket and allowed the lock to suck it in. The key turned by itself and the door opened. She said goodbye to Stella and she and Bentley stepped inside.

Once inside with the door locked, the bookcase on the back wall slid up into the ceiling and the old workshop beckoned. They were greeted by the rich aroma of coffee coming from a king-sized coffee machine bubbling away on a desk which also held cups and plates of cookies. Adept Babbage, dressed in an immaculate pinstripe suit, turned from the machine with a steaming cup in his hand.

"You're here," he said with a worried look. "Either of you seen Perry?"

As if on cue there was loud rapping on the front door. Bentley went to answer it and returned with a panting Perry.

"Sorry I am late, Adept Babbage," he said. "I overslept." He fell into a chair and caught his breath.

"Overslept?" Babbage raised an eyebrow. "The most important day in the history of humanity and you oversleep?"

"I am sorry, sir. I – I had – I had a restless night."

"And your tulpa, is she not gracing us with her ghostly presence?"

Perry looked to the floor, wiped his eyes. "No sir, I've given her the day off."

"Tulpas have permission to be present, as you well know. Is it not wiser to have that second head thinking for you?"

There was an awkward silence as Babbage and Perry stared at each other. Perry had a nervous look, as if he was expecting the worst. "To be honest, sir," he eventually said. "She was getting anxious… about not being allowed into the blip. So I – well, I ordered her to lie down until I returned."

Babbage grunted. In the space that had once contained General Cohn's Starburst was a long table. Chairs had been positioned to one side. Babbage indicated them to take a seat, which they did. Babbage's clown emerged from the back wall and began serving coffee and cookies.

A tartan blanket covered the table's bulky contents and behind it stood an easel covered with a similar blanket. Babbage stood next to the easel. "In less than an hour," he said, "the trial of Kimi Jo Nichols will begin." The clown had finished serving. Babbage waved it away and it vanished into the wall. "However, we must not view this as a trial."

"Why not?" Bentley said. "Because that's what it is."

"Certainly not." Babbage held his head high. "Balancer Nichols has proved to be a truthful soul of the highest order. The evidence she returns with will clear her immediately. I have no doubt about that. So, my friends, and especially you, Kimi. You must view this as a *mission* – not a trial - and a simple one at that." He pulled the blanket from the easel and a white board was revealed.

On it were bullet points.

1) *Enter blip.*
2) *Tame fear.*
3) *Perry to operate the twister.*
4) *Exit blip.*
5) *Produce evidence.*
6) *NOT GUILTY!*
7) *MISSION COMPLETE!*

"What's a twister?" Bentley asked.

Babbage reached into his breast pocket and pulled out a small hourglass. He held it up between his thumb and finger. "Big Sue's oven-timer. Using Kimi's DNA, the sand particles within have been programmed to restart the jump once the fear has been tamed and collected."

The sand within the hourglass seemed to twinkle at Kimi. "Clever," she said.

"An oven-timer?" Bentley looked unsure.

"It *has* been thoroughly tested, Tulpa Bentley. Worry not. It is foolproof."

Bentley took a bite of cookie.

Kimi thought the brown chips on the cookies looked like the doo-doos they'd tasted at the library. Bentley looked at her, nodded, took another bite.

"It is time to reveal the device and its workings." Babbage took hold of the blanket covering the table's contents and whipped it away.

Bentley said: "That's a device?"

Babbage had uncovered a pair of bright red traffic cones, a roll of black tape, a tiny plastic sofa from a doll's house, two lengths of stiff wire and a large dodo's egg which, judging by the two small holes in it, had been emptied of its contents.

"Apologies for the crudeness," Babbage said. "Rules of the court - greylian law forbids us from having a working model or even a graphic to use for this briefing. We are not even allowed to keep this crude version assembled, should wrong eyes be watching." Babbage smiled. "Perry will now give a demonstration."

Perry, slouching in the chair to Kimi's right, eyes closed in concentration, did not move.

"Perry!"

Perry jumped.

"The demonstration please."

Perry got up, walked slowly around the table, one hand touching it as he went, eyeing up the various pieces. He was wearing the blue overalls he wore at the dodo farm and a bright green t-shirt, and his hair looked flat and his face drawn and tired. Expecting him to shoot her a glance, Kimi felt her cheeks warming. But he did not look up. On reaching Babbage's side he closed his eyes once more.

"Are you all right, boy?" Babbage said.

"Thinking, sir - just thinking. I want to get this right."

"Get it right? You've done it a hundred times in practice."

"Last minute nerves," Bentley said. "Seen it all before."

Perry's eyes opened. "I'm ready." He smiled his white smile, took the roll of black tape and, starting from the base of one traffic cone, he rolled out the tape, pressing it into place as he moved around the cone and upwards to its tip creating a spiralling effect. "Like a helter-skelter," he said brightly.

After murmurs of agreement he repeated the process on the second cone. Positioning the cones about a metre apart, he took the two straight pieces of wire, stuck one in the top of each cone then bent them towards each other in a smooth arc before finally placing the free ends into the two small holes in the dodo's egg, which now bobbed precariously in the air between the two cones.

"This may look rather unsophisticated," Babbage said. "But the real deal is something else."

"How does it work?" Kimi asked.

Perry, staring at the contraption, did not look overly sure.

"Get on with it," Babbage said.

"Okay, okay." Perry picked up the tiny plastic sofa, placed it at the base of the cone on the left, and stared at it.

"Mojo, Perry – mojo!"

They waited. Perry stared at the toy sofa.

"I might remind you," Babbage said to Kimi, "That mojo does not work inside the blip!"

"Looks like it doesn't work here either," Bentley said. "If you ask me the lad's not firing on all cylinders."

Perry was staring hard at the toy sofa. "It's all right," he said. "Just warming up."

The tiny plastic sofa trembled then began to move, slowly following the spiralling line of black tape on its upward journey around the traffic cone.

"Commentary!" Babbage reminded.

"Yes, yes, sorry. The chair is going up and around, as you can see. Like going backwards up a helter-skelter. And soon it will enter the erm, the blip, yes – which is the dodo's egg in the middle, where it – *we* – will stop, and..."

Babbage stepped up to the table, plucked the toy sofa from the cone. "Sit down, boy, and get some coffee. You need to be sharp for this mission."

"You should send Chief Rehd instead," Bentley said. "I'd feel a whole lot better."

"The greylians would not allow it," Babbage said. "Perry has been thoroughly tested and proved to be the perfect candidate. He has no fear! We therefore must press on as planned. *I* will demonstrate."

Babbage placed the toy sofa back at the base of the cone on the left, pinged it with a finger and the thing shot around the lines of black tape, spiralled up the cone, travelled along the arc of wire and vanished inside the dodo's egg with a flourish of twinkling mojo. The dodo egg bobbed on its wires and glowed.

"It's that simple," Babbage said. "Kimi and Perry will be strapped into a chair, shot up the helter-skelter contraption at high speed, travel the wire until it reaches halfway between the two helter-skelters where it is programmed to halt inside the dodo's egg."

"The blip," Kimi said.

"That's right." Babbage held up the hourglass timer. "Once inside the blip you will locate and tame your fear and then Perry will twist the time-twister, like this..." Babbage twisted the timer. The dodo egg shattered and the toy sofa sped along the second wire, entered the spiralling black tape on the second cone and spun all the way to the bottom before shooting off the table and towards Kimi who snatched it from the air.

"Of course, there will be mojo buffers on the real contraption which will stop the chair safely at the bottom. Your very own mentor, Stella is assigned to buffer creation."

"That's neat," Kimi said.

"How long will they be in the blip?" asked Bentley.

"Good question," Babbage said. "But one I cannot answer. From personal experience, my best estimate is that Kimi could find and tame her fear within as little as five minutes.

But it may take an hour. We just don't know. For those of us observing the jump, there will of course be no delay at all. Those watching will see a change in the air, possibly wavering, but not for long. When Perry uses the twister the chair will reappear and return to us *back* in time – which is set precisely one second before the chair leaves."

"Which means we will actually come back before we have left," Kimi said.

"Absolutely correct," Babbage said.

"And the doppelganger paradox won't kick in because of the groan time," Kimi added.

"Right again," Babbage smiled approvingly. "I'm pleased someone is on the ball!"

"What is groan time?" Perry said. He took a sip of coffee.

Kimi looked at him. "Groan time. Last time I did this we used two twirlies, as per Dad's formula. But here, Dad will have, erm…" She couldn't find the word.

"Mimicked?" Babbage offered.

"Yeah, that. And because it works like a twirly it will have groan time like a twirly, and as long as we enter the blip before we meet ourselves coming back, we won't explode."

"Implode, you mean implode," Babbage said.

"Whatever," Kimi shrugged. "Guess it hurts either way."

Babbage gave her a nod. "Any more questions?"

"Yes," Bentley said. "When they get back. What then?"

"Kimi will stand before the judge and the director of proceedings, summon her tamed fear, and in turn the fear will open its head and reveal what really happened on the day General Cohn and his ship disappeared."

"And the judge will believe what he sees?"

"Oh yes. Both the judge and the director of proceedings have been involved with preparations all the way, have witnessed my own clown pulling its head apart, and are in no doubt about its worth as evidence. The judge will accept whatever Kimi's fear reveals as the truth and nothing but the truth, and hopefully the director of proceedings will be satisfied."

"Who is the judge?" Bentley asked.

"I cannot divulge that. But I can say that this judge has arbitrated disputes for many years and has the respect of many worlds. A judge that can be trusted."

"Fair enough. Where is the trial taking place?"

"Mission!" Babbage corrected. He checked his watch. "We'll be leaving shortly so I suppose I can reveal that now." He began dismantling the model. "Kimi and Perry's mission will take place on Bodmin Moor."

"On Earth?" Bentley said. "Is that wise?"

"We had little choice, Tulpa Bentley. The greylians demanded neutral ground. We are fortunate they agreed to Bodmin Moor – or to be more precise: *The Hurlers*."

"I know them," Kimi said. "Three stone circles high on the moor. Dad used to sketch them. I first met Bentley not far from there."

"That you did," Bentley said. "Bodmin Moor is a magical place."

You said magic, Kimi thought.

Bentley smiled, then said dreamily: "Bodmin Moor, where the true magic runs close beneath the Earth's surface, where evil fears to tread, where the very heart of the old mystic yearns to be, where witches and warlocks have toiled for centuries and…"

"All right," Babbage cut in. "Let's not get all dramatic."

"What about the people who live on the moor?" Kimi asked. "They're gonna notice two great helter-skelters."

"Not many live on Bodmin Moor," Babbage said. "But those that do are all balancers."

"All of them? Wow!"

"Apart from one or two adepts and a home for retired monkeys, yes, every one. On top of that, all roads and rambling paths have been closed, as has the airspace for a fifty-kilometre radius. We can be certain that when you return with your fear you will do so with the utmost privacy, security, and protection. Which reminds me – your fear – the monster under the bed thing – what are your latest thoughts on that?"

Kimi shrugged. "I can't see there being a problem. I'll poke it in the eye and be back in a jiffy."

"Now there's a point," Bentley said. "Kimi has never set eyes on this monster thing. What if it doesn't have any eyes?"

"That is a good point," Babbage said. "But poking your fear in the eye is merely an expression. When Kimi finds her man with a hundred hands she must stand up to him, be firm, be insistent, be unafraid. Do it convincingly and she will have tamed her fear."

"I see," Bentley said.

"And you, Kimi? You understand what you have to do?" Kimi nodded.

"Good. Now, there is one last thing," Babbage said.

This isn't good news, Kimi thought.

No it isn't, Bentley's thought came back loud and clear.

"When I said your parents refused to leave the device for fear of tampering hands, well, that was not strictly true."

"I had a feeling about that," Bentley said.

Kimi could not take her eyes off Babbage. "Where are they?"

"They are there on the moor with the device. I do not mean to scare you, simply that you must know the truth before we leave." Somewhere outside a crow cawed. "And the thing of it is," Babbage went on. "The greylians wanted some security, a guarantee if you like. They insisted Kimi's parents remain on site, and, in the event that Kimi does not show willing to attend her trial, they would at least have some leverage to get her there."

"So they're been held there," Bentley said.

"That stinks," Kimi said.

"True," Babbage said. "Your parents are safe and well, but you must realise that although they will be there, I'm afraid you will not be reunited with them until after the mission is complete."

"Reunited?"

"He means no hugs until the trial's over," Bentley said.

"Do you feel all right, Kimi?" Babbage asked.

Her arms were hot and itchy where the bandages bound her freaky quills. The ridiculous spurs wrapped to her legs had grown some more – they were getting heavy, and it felt like she was wearing big boots. One of the Elastoplast patches on her nose must have come partly away because she could feel a slight rush of air with every breath. This seemed to lift her energy, a lift she might need judging by Perry's poor performance. He hadn't said much, was acting too nervous and Kimi had some inkling that she would be the one looking after him. She took a deep breath, enjoyed the cold rush of air, stood up. "Yes, I feel more than all right."

"And you, Perry?" Babbage said. "Have you woken up yet?"

Perry got to his feet. "Yes Adept Babbage, sir. I am fine now."

"Then you will need this," Babbage gave him the time-twister. "Successful completion of this mission is paramount, Balancer Sunder. Failure is not an option."

"I will not fail, sir."

Babbage gave him one last stare. Or was it a glare? Kimi was not sure.

For the sake of old times and precious memories, Bentley insisted he be the one to twirly them through dimensions to the Earth space of Bodmin Moor. Disappointed that he was not allowed to land them in the cornfield where he and Kimi had met, he made a short speech anyway. A speech that Kimi did not hear a lot of because Perry had come to her side, had a hand on her shoulder, and his mouth so close to her ear she could feel the warmth of his breath.

"*I have you an answer…*" Perry whispered. The loose Elastoplast on her nose made a slight flutter. "*…of course, darling Kimi, we shall be married.*"

"…And God bless all who sail in her!" Bentley said.

There was scraping of furniture as space was made, Bentley's grinning face as he twirled the air, and backs were patted as Kimi was shuffled, heart booming into the twirly.

***

12
Phenate Thrawn

Perry's weird words rang in her mind like ridiculous wedding bells and Kimi was glad when the fizzling started. She closed her ears to the sound of disassembling human atoms, closed her eyes to the milky white void as dimensions were crossed, and did not open them again until her feet landed on soft ground and a chill touched her cheeks.

The grey-blue twilight of early morning held still over Bodmin Moor. They were on a hillock overlooking three huge stone circles; dampened with dew, each stone uniquely gnarled and twisted, each resonating a hum through the air that could be felt in the bones.

"This is a good place to be," Bentley said.

Kimi had expected to see two huge helter-skelters built over the stone circles, but there were no structures, only people and greylians on scaffolding seating outside the circles and tall lighting rigs lending an eerie glow to the dawn air. A greylian craft was parked on the grass beyond; small, black, triangular, white lights blinking at its extremities. Kimi guessed that might be her transport out of here if she was found guilty.

Three army buses stood in a row to the left of the stone

circles alongside seven or eight army jeeps. Fifty or more armed soldiers as well as greylians with weapons were walking among the stone circles. This surprised Kimi. She had expected the fuzz to be here, not the army. A greylian figure emerged from the crowd below and came sashaying up the hillock. It wore a blue tunic which stopped at its knees. Wrinkles beneath eyes that were not the usual glossy black but seemed fogged or faded told Kimi this was an old greylian.

"I am Tunahmee," it said in a soft feminine whisper, "Director of proceedingssssss."

Babbage bowed. "Tunahmee, it's good to see you again." Then to Kimi: "Tunahmee is here on my request. She is as knowledgeable of Earth mythology as she is of greylian authority. She is witness and director of proceedings, which means she has your best interests at heart."

Kimi did not bow. "Where are my parents?"

Tunahmee pointed a bony finger to the black triangular craft. "If guilty, you will join your parentssssss."

"Kimi is *not* guilty," Bentley said sternly.

"It's all right," Babbage said. "Your mother and father are safe on board the craft. The greylians insist on no contact until the evidence has been given. They will be released as soon as the judge decrees you innocent. I'm sorry, Kimi, but that's the way it is."

Kimi looked at the black craft, could feel the eyes of Mum and Dad, watching. Mum would have her fingers crossed. She raised a hand in a wave.

A sudden gust of wind drew everyone's attention. Behind Tunahmee a wide and ferocious vortex opened. It dispersed with a blast of throbbing engine and rattling mudguards as a chrome squad bike turned a circle and sprayed up sods of turf. Chief Rehd, in camouflage gear, stilled the engine, climbed down, then helped Stella from the back seat.

Stella came to Kimi's side, put an arm around her

shoulder.

"I'm glad you're on buffer duty," Kimi said.

"Don't worry," Stella said, "I'll make it a good one."

Kimi noted Perry staring out at the three huge stone circles. He looked apprehensive, maybe even scared.

Rehd gave Tunahmee a salute. "When do the fireworks start?"

"When all are pressssssent," the greylian scanned the scene below, "Which seemsssss like now." She turned back to Kimi and Perry. "Come, it is time to build the device."

"Good luck, Kimi." Bentley had tears in his eyes.

Kimi looked to Babbage.

"It's alright, Kimi," Babbage nodded. "Go with Tunahmee."

Stella smiled her gap-toothed smile. "See you in a jiffy, sister. Hurry back!"

Kimi was hesitant. Babbage came, rested a hand on her shoulder. "The device is there waiting, Kimi. We are about to witness one of mankind's greatest achievements at work."

"We are?"

"We certainly are. You are about to meet old Thrawn of Stones. Have you heard of her, Kimi?"

"No sir, I haven't heard of her."

"Phenate Thrawn is an Adept Supreme, an Elemental Balancer, so advanced that she can only survive by blending with the elements. Witnessing an elemental at work can be both amazing and alarming at the same time."

There was a noticeable change in the air as the humming from the stones intensified. The soldiers and greylians within the stone circles were moving quickly to the outsides.

"Some say staring Phenate in the eyes will turn you into the very stone she controls, but that is merely myth. Phenate might appear mad, but she is here for the good, always the good, never the evil. Okay?"

Kimi nodded, took a deep breath, let it out slowly, and

was just telling herself to focus when golden sunlight burst from the horizon and speared across the moor. A soft breeze lifted Kimi's hair. Little Hand tingled, mojo ready, yet it was mojo that could not be used. She wondered if Little Hand would tingle once inside the blip. At Kimi's side, Perry swayed, steadied himself.

"Balancer Sunder?" Babbage gripped his arm.

"I – I feel a bit sick, sir."

"It's only nerves, boy. Pull yourself together."

Little Hand tingled again. This was not the brave Perry that Kimi had expected.

"Phenate is an eccentric," Babbage went on. "Some say she's crazy, but whatever anyone might say about Phenate Thrawn, let me tell you, she is a wonder to behold."

Clouds dispersed quickly, revealing soft blue sky and a dozen or more greylian ships which backed away with haste until they blinked out of sight.

"So much for the closed airspace," Bentley said.

"She's clever," Babbage said. "Now, are you ready, Kimi?"

Kimi nodded.

"Then go with Tunahmee."

The frail greylian smiled, offered a knobbled hand.

Kimi took Tunahmee's bony fingers in hers; fingers so long they wrapped round Kimi's hand. The greylian offered the other hand to Perry, who looked away to the stone circles. "I'm ready," he said, then set off down the slope clutching the hourglass.

Tunahmee shrugged and headed down the slope with Kimi holding tight to the greylian's hand.

"Bring it back, sister!" Stella shouted.

Kimi's heart thumped. The grass was damp with dew. Not wanting to slip and take the greylian down with her, Kimi trod carefully.

"Watch your back!" Rehd's voice.

"I'm with you!" Bentley's shout.

The breeze that had cleared the clouds came down in a swirl. The crowds in the scaffolding seats hushed. Those army vehicles with running engines coughed and spluttered and died. The generators running the lights puttered to a stop and the lights went out. There was absolute silence. The only thing left with power appeared to be the black triangular craft; the white lights at its tips still blinking.

Tunahmee and Kimi continued towards the central of the three stone circles. Tunahmee brought them to a stop next to a standing stone that leaned to the right and was twice the height of Kimi.

"We are ready," Tunahmee said to the air.

This close to the stones, their song was more vibrant. Kimi could feel it through the soles of her feet; a vibrancy growing in pitch to the sound of unseen flutes or pipes that seemed to haunt the air around them. Then there was movement within the circle, near its middle where a single small stone, which looked out of place, began to turn in an anticlockwise direction, growing, stirring up soil and screwing itself from the earth. When the stone reached a height greater than the ones in the circle the sunlight struck its tip. A loud crack echoed across the moor and the stone began to split and peel open as if it were a blooming flower, revealing within a tall and bulky figure cloaked within a monk's brown robe; its head covered by a large cowl. The crowd gasped as one.

The stone shuddered and the peeling stopped. The robed figure floated from its centre and moved silently through the air towards Tunahmee who took a step forward. The greylian held its long arms wide and the robed figure floated into its enfolding embrace. Locked in this strange hug, they remained still as the sound of the pipes in the air diminished and the hum of the stones returned. Tunahmee opened her arms and the robed figure drew back, settled to the grass, and pulled back the cowl.

Three words: "Phenate is here..." whispered through the

gathered crowds. Kimi even heard them escape her own lips. "Phenate is here…"

The woman appeared young yet grotesque; features puckered and twisted, hair a straggle of brambles festooned with spiders and cobwebs. A grin that split her face from ear to ear made her look like a horror show puppet, but it was the eyes that got Kimi – red glittering eyes, the like of which she had seen once before in the darkness of the Shed's 'lift'.

Phenate's grin disappeared. She stared at Kimi, pursed her lips and blew with force. A strong breeze that smelled of garlic washed over Kimi. "Hello again," the woman said.

Kimi felt herself smiling.

The woman looked Perry up and down. She untied her robe and let it drop to the ground. Her shoulders appeared to be constructed of interwoven branches, solid and thick from which vines trailed into tendrils, dressing her with spade-shaped leaves in various purples and shimmering golds that moved as she moved and clung tight to her form. Charcoal black legs that could have been fire-damaged sticks on delicate feet stepped carefully towards Perry - who looked terrified.

"You know me?" she said in a voice that was strained yet soft and beautiful.

Perry's eyes were wide. He was shaking his head. Kimi noticed Phenate's heart beating, pumping the leaves on her chest.

"Nooooooooooo?" Phenate said, dramatically forlorn. She looked to the ground and let out a sigh that stank of garlic. She snapped her head back up. "Never mind," she said, then sprang to the air and danced around inside the stone circle emitting a soulful cry like the mewl of a new-born kitten, and as she danced and whirled, the mewls became words and the singing was beautiful…

Oh my things, you are love-ly, lovelier than air be, oh my things you are love-ly…

And the stones hummed along.

...lovelier than maybe, oh my things, oh my things...

And the crowd hummed, even the soldiers - and Kimi found herself humming.

...you are lovely, lovely, lovelier than honey-bees, oh my things, oh my things...

She's mad, Kimi thought.

She's Welsh, Bentley's thought came right back, *and a damn fine warbler*, he added.

...oh my things... and Phenate Thrawn leapt to the air with a spin and landed in the centre of the peeled stone flower from which she had emerged. She looked to the sky, raised her hands. She no longer sang but her tune seemed to hang in the air as the ground around her began to shake and rumble. From beneath the earth, more stone, solid yet fluid at the same time, pushed free from the soil, raising Phenate and the stone flower until a stage was formed beneath them complete with rough stone steps.

...oh my things, oh my things, Phenate stretched her arms wide, fingers pointing to the two outer stone circles. These stones were moving now, lifting from the earth, dragging themselves towards each circle's middle, scraping mass over mass, building, forming a conical shape with thuds and thumps and cracks and bangs and Kimi realised the helter-skelters were being formed.

From beyond the two outer circles, more stones, each as big as a car, were pushing through the soil, sprouting like giants' gravestones. The ground beneath Kimi's feet was trembling. One army jeep overturned, and then another as stones birthed themselves from the ground beneath them and rolled them over with ease. Soldiers and greylians fled as the ground they stood on shook and trembled and blocks of dark stone emerged, each tumbling into place with a thud and a thump as if moved by some invisible hand. Thump and thud, thump and thud, the huge stones, dozens of them, made their way to the two growing structures, scraping and climbing and sliding their way to the top of each, until at last the two enormous structures were complete, each as tall as three houses.

...oh my things, oh my things, oh my things please be good to me, better than hair maybe – oh my things, oh my things... Phenate went silent, satin-red eyes glittering, mouth twisted into the strangest smile. With a flourish of her arms and a violent shake of her torso which sent her shock of bramble hair into a rattling frenzy, the most amazing thing happened; from beneath the feathery tendrils and flapping leaves that made her form, a little white dog sprang free. As shaggy as its owner, the yelping thing scampered and leaped and bounced into Kimi's arms.

"Is the girl good to go?" Phenate shouted from her rocky perch.

The dog looked into Kimi's eyes, and Kimi could have sworn she saw it smile. A fat pink tongue licked her face.

"Blossom says yes," Phenate said, and the dog somersaulted to the ground, and before bounding back to Phenate, it raised a leg and peed on the bare shins of a greylian soldier. "Sorry 'bout that," Phenate said. "But you guys do look awfully like trees."

This brought a chuckle from the watching crowds.

Phenate raised her arms to the air once more, eyes glittering like laser beams. She sucked in a great breath. "Are you ready for your mission, oh secret one?"

She means you! - Bentley's thought.

"Yes, yes," Kimi said, pleased that her voice wasn't shaky. "Very ready."

The little white dog Phenate had referred to as Blossom raised a paw in Kimi's direction before springing to the air and burying itself among Phenate's leafy attire.

Phenate winked. "Then let's bring it on, twig!" Phenate began to vibrate. Her clothes of leaf and vine and tendril were shaking themselves into a blur, the leaves lifting as if blown by some internal breeze. Kimi half-expected to see the white dog come tumbling out but what did emerge was an awesome sight.

Hundreds of shimmering famoose spheres emerged in two streams of rainbow light. One after the other in quick succession they flew, clicking their speedy wings, to the opposing structures and encircling them in spirals that gave the appearance of a chute to each of the `helter-skelters`.

One famoose paused in front of Kimi. She kept her mouth firmly closed and held out the back of a hand. The sphere settled, clicking wings stopped and unfolded. The rodent, its eyes fierce and red, smiled its bucktoothed smile. "Remember me?" it said in a tinny voice. "There's exactly fifteen-thousand of us this time, Kimi. We won't let you down."

"Thanks," she said and the famoose took flight and joined the streams of light. To Tunahmee, Kimi said: "I was told my dad designed this device?"

"Oh yesssss," Tunahmee said. "You father is a geniusssss. Your mum is not bad either." Tunahmee smiled.

"But it's hardly a device. Just rocks and famoose."

"You expected to see science, but you see nature instead, Kimi – the device of nature is more accurate than sciencccccce."

Two soldiers hurried by, carrying what looked like the back seat from a car, complete with seat belts. Kimi spotted a cloud-shaped stain on the seat, one she had made when she puked chocolate milkshake on the way from McDonald's. The soldiers placed the seat at the base of the rock structure on the left – just like Perry had placed the doll-house sofa at the base of the traffic cone. The structure pulled the seat to itself so that its rungs rested on the two lanes of whirring famoose, where it swayed gently.

Kimi was about to voice the fact that Perry looked

worryingly pale, and that this ride into the blip might make him throw up really badly, when Phenate shouted: "All stand for the judge!"

The sound of a helicopter's thrumming blades made everyone look to the sky.

The helicopter was a rich maroon colour and had a golden crest on its side. The low sun glinted off its windows. It landed on the grass behind the centre circle. On the raised stone stage, Phenate turned to face it. Kimi could not see what was going on because the stage blocked her view, but the crowds in the scaffolding were getting excited. The helicopter's engine went silent and its rotor blades slowed to a stop. A soldier came onto the stage from the other side, carrying an ornate chair with a plump red cushion. He placed it to one side of Phenate and then stood to attention.

The first Kimi saw of the judge was the bobbled dome of pink with feathers and pins sticking from it. This turned out to be a hat, and when Kimi saw the kind face beneath it she could not quite believe her eyes. She had seen this face many times before… *on stamps and coins.*

Phenate curtseyed, and the judge, in a stunning pink coat to match the hat nodded her thanks and sat herself in the plush chair. She was joined by two little brown dogs which lay at her feet.

"That's the judge?" Kimi whispered to Tunahmee.

"Yesssss," Tunahmee whispered back.

"Charlie said it would be a greylian judge."

"It is," Tunahmee said. "But you must be silent now. Listen to the judge."

The lady in pink waved a white-gloved hand and the soldier beckoned them forward. Tunahmee took Kimi's hand and they went to the stage with Perry bringing up the rear and stood on the first stone step. Tunahmee curtseyed. Kimi attempted the same but nearly fell over when Perry also dropped *his* knees into a curtsey. Murmurs of laughter came from the crowd.

"I wear pink today," the judge began, "because I know it is your favourite colour, Kimi. And I believe, despite being judge on this momentous occasion, that Kimi Nichols will bring good news from the beyond."

"Thank you," Kimi said.

"Now, may I wish you both the very best of luck, and promise me you won't bring any of those horrid bliss flies back with you, otherwise one will be a goner!"

Kimi giggled.

"Good. Let proceedings commence!"

Phenate, who had been still and quiet during this discourse, made the deepest curtsey before throwing her arms to the air once more. Once again came the distant melodic sound of flutes and pipes. The stones hummed loudly. The famoose whirred into motion, furious wing-clicks matching the vibration in the stones.

"It will be perfect," Tunahmee said, addressing Kimi and Perry with a slender grey hand on each. "Travellers through time and space, please take your seatsssss."

Ushered to the old car seat by two uniformed guards and a pair of greylians with rocket launchers, Kimi realised she was not nervous. As the seatbelt was stretched across her chest and clunked into place by a greylian hand, Kimi felt calm and peaceful. Perry, on the other hand, was a trembling wreck. She took his hand. It felt cold and clammy.

"This is crazy," he said. "Crazy, crazy, crazy."

"We'll be fine," Kimi said. "Back in a jiffy. You'll see."

"I hope you are worth it," he mumbled.

"What?"

Perry closed his eyes.

Kimi could no longer see the judge, or Phenate, but she could hear Phenate's music, hear her words. She thought of Mum and Dad watching from the black craft and promised to do them proud. From the hillock, Bentley and Babbage were waving. Chief Rehd had come down the slope and was chatting to a soldier. He caught Kimi's eye and gave a proud and firm salute.

Tunahmee brought a small bell from her tunic and rang it. The crowds, the soldiers, all went quiet. Only the sweet singing of Phenate could be heard. "Thisssss," Tunahmee said, her old grey eyes wide and staring at Kimi, "Isssss the moment of truth. When you enter the blip you may be away for some time, but for usssss, you will return before you leave." Tunahmee nodded in the direction of the second stone tower.

Both Kimi and Perry turned their heads to see greylian and army soldiers gathering at the base of the structure where Stella was weaving green mist from her hands into a thick and comfy mojo crash-mat.

"Your return will be ssssswift. Do you undersssssstand?"

"Yes!" Perry said sharply.

"Got it," Kimi said.

Tunahmee smiled. "As director of proceedingsssss, I must remind you that it is not only the judge you have to pleasssssse. If there are any doubtsssss about your evidence then I have the power to waive."

"Wave?" Kimi said.

"To stay the judgement," Tunahmee said. "Perhapsssss even to declare you guilty."

"Okay," Kimi said, not liking this development.

It's all right, Kimi - Bentley's thought - *Tunahmee is just crossing her T's.*

"You are ready?" Tunahmee was at the side of their seat.

"I'm ready," Kimi said.

She squeezed Perry's damp hand. "Yes, yes," he said. "Hurry up, please."

Tunahmee slid backwards, signalled to Phenate whose singing quietened to a stop, and a hush fell over the moor.

"Famoooooooooooosssssse!" came Phenate's voice.

"Preparrrrrrrre for launch!" The famoose whirred as one, the car seat bobbed comfortably on their droning wings. Kimi heard Perry swallow and wished they'd brought sick bags.

"Stones of Thrawn!" Phenate's voice again. The stones rumbled and tightened their positions. Trickles of soil pattered around them.

"On five, my lovelies!" Phenate shouted.

Tunahmee bowed and slinked further away. "Good luck!"

"On four, beautiful things, on four!"

The two lines of famoose running like tracks before them and spiralling off around the stone tower glowed in myriad colours. Kimi looked up to where the mountain of stones pointed skyward and the twin trails of shimmering famoose buzzed and clicked and whirred and waited to thrust them into oblivion. She held onto Perry's arm.

"THREE!" The crowd had joined in with the countdown now.

Kimi closed her eyes.

"TWO!"

The old car seat went still. The famoose were focusing.

"LAUNCH!!!"

The wind came hard in Kimi's face, pummelled her cheeks, pulled at her hair. The force of the rapid ascent around the spiral of famoose pulled both Kimi and Perry in towards the stones. Kimi heard a strange jabbering noise and opened her eyes right at the point where the seat left the tip of the tower and witnessed the vomit erupting from Perry's quivering lips and flying off behind. A heartbeat later Bodmin Moor vanished into whiteness and vomit began to fizzle and break up just as Perry's face grew holes which expanded into other holes and then Kimi's own eyes fizzled away their vision and there she floated among the white for a while, with no body, with no weight, just floating in the silence until the fizzling started again and the vomit came to rest on Perry's face and in his hair.

"I'm sorry," he said. He looked awful.

***

13
'One death today'

Arrival was unexpectedly abrupt. The old car seat was no longer with them. Perry had fallen to his knees into black mud. With her knees bent, Kimi's feet hit the ground and she yelped in surprise but the yelp was dulled by drizzling rain and oppressive darkness. It was night-time, the air warm and damp. They were surrounded by vines and tropical leaves and upturned stumps with roots that curled like greylian fingers, dripping with sticky webs of unseen spiders.

"This must be the jungle Adept Babbage talked about," Perry said.

"We need to search," Kimi said. Perry agreed and they moved forward, pushing through wet leathery leaves.

"I can hear bliss flies," Perry said. "Listen!"

Kimi listened. "I can't." She moved on.

"Wait, Kimi, if there's bliss flies we need to avoid them."

Kimi turned. "Why? Neither of us is wearing pink. Unless, erm."

"No Kimi, I'm not wearing pink, I just don't like bliss flies."

"You're frightened of them?"

"I didn't say that."

"You're meant to be fearless. That's why you're here. To help me beat my fear."

"And I will help you. I am fearless. Bliss flies just give - give me – make me – panicky, that's all."

Kimi grinned at him.

"What?"

She made her hand into a fist. "Bliss flies are this big," she said, recalling the time Bentley had done the very same to her.

"I know how big they are."

"Yesssss," Kimi hissed. "This big, fat, white and plump with eggs."

Perry took a step back.

Kimi ran at him, twisting her fist this way and that and all the while hissing "*Blisssss*."

Perry fell over, panting.

Kimi stopped at his feet. "I'm worried," she said.

Perry got up. Both of them were soaked from the drizzle and Perry's hair was flat.

"Maybe it's the rain you can hear hitting the leaves. Sounds a bit like a bliss hiss."

Perry was shaking his head. "I hear them, Kimi. And I'm not afraid. I'd simply rather not be near them. Horrid things. Can we please just get going and find this bed monster of yours?"

Perry's eyes went horribly wide. Kimi spun her head round to see the first bliss flies arrive. But these weren't big-as-fists bliss flies, these were nightmare bliss flies, each the size of a large melon, plump and round; their skin a translucent pearly white beneath which their eggs swirled in gloopy fluids ready to be pumped into anything pink.

There were hundreds of bliss flies. The presence of so many bobbing luminescent monstrosities seemed to bring some brightness to this dank jungle but their noise was penetrating, irritating, annoying.

Blisssss. Blisssss. Blisssss.

Perry ran past Kimi with his hands on his ears and his eyes on stalks.

Kimi followed, bashing through bliss flies on the way, slapping through soaked undergrowth and spider's webs glistening with water droplets which clung to her face and made her splutter.

Perry had stopped. He was holding back a branch laden with floppy wet leaves. "Look!"

Kimi reached his side. They were looking at a red-brick wall that seemed to be sitting on its own in the darkness. It had a white door and two small frosted windows that glowed with light from within.

"Is this your house?" Perry said, moving forward.

"No," Kimi said, batting a bliss fly and following. Then she realised what it was – or at least what it was meant to be. A hot band of fear seared the inside of her chest. Her breath caught. She'd stopped walking.

"Kimi," Perry said. "You have a bliss fly on your head."

Kimi could feel its feet in her hair. She closed her eyes. "I am not afraid," she said.

"Kimi?"

She batted the bliss fly away and strode toward the white door, clutched the handle.

"What is it, Kimi?"

"It's the school toilets. I should have known. They give me the willies. Don't know why. But they do."

There was a sudden drone of many bliss flies. Perry put his hand on hers, pressed the handle, and pushed Kimi inside. He closed the door just as the flies bumped against it. Some went to the frosted windows either side of the door and nudged against them like fuzzy clouds.

They were in a single room, narrow but long. Three more frosted windows sat in each wall, each window situated above a toilet cubicle. All the cubicle doors were closed. More hazy bliss flies had made their way to these windows and were knocking gently against them. There were two porcelain sinks, both cracked, broken and dripping rusty water to the tiled floor. Some tiles were missing, others cracked or loose. An earwig crawled from a tap and dropped into the nearest sink. Another scuttled across the floor, disappearing into a small bunch of fungi that looked like miniature mushrooms which sprouted from black mould in various places where floor met wall. Fluorescent strip lights ran in a single row up the long ceiling. One was dead, the rest buzzed and flickered.

"What kind of school do you go to?" Perry asked.

"My school loos are nothing like this. Well, they have the same sinks and windows and the same cubicles with the same colour doors but none of the creepy-mouldy-drippy-insecty stuff going on."

"So your fear exaggerates the effect?"

"I guess."

"Well there's no bed in here. We should try the next door." Perry indicated to the door in the far wall.

Staring at the door, wondering if she would find her bed in the room beyond with the Gribbley Grabbley Monster snuffling underneath, Kimi heard a soft breathing sound. "Listen!"

Perry gazed towards the cubicles. "I hear it," he whispered.

"Come out!" Kimi shouted, which made Perry jump.

Her shout brought the bliss flies into a frenzy, thumping noisily against the windows, hissing more harshly and drowning any sound that might be coming from the cubicles.

"Come out!" she shouted again.

To their left, the door of the middle cubicle made a creak as it opened a couple of inches. Perry stepped in front of Kimi. "I'll handle this."

Outside, thunder rumbled, lightning flashed, rain lashed so hard it could be heard pounding the walls. The strip lights flickered rapidly and all went out apart from the one near the far door.

"Scary," Kimi said.

"Don't worry, it's obviously special effects, created by your fear," Perry said.

Kimi knew he was right, but she stayed behind Perry as the cubicle door opened a little further.

"Come out please," she said.

The door swung inwards. A dark figure emerged which had the appearance of a glossy shadow. Lighting flashed, adding light to the form and highlighting the features of a girl; a girl with long black hair who looked identical to Kimi. She wore a jagged cape which hung to just above her knees, along with pointed black boots; both of these things more suited to a comic book hero. The girl smiled and silver fangs glinted. She stepped forward, emitting a throaty hiss that sounded much worse than any bliss fly. Perry took a step back and made to say something but the girl moved and in a blink she was right before him. She raised a finger with a blackened nail and licked her black lips. The fingernail grew in front of Perry's face and the girl touched it to his neck.

Perry fainted. Kimi caught him, stumbled backwards, and they both fell to the floor.

"Where is my prey?" the girl said.

Kimi stared at the freaky version of herself. "You're me?"

"I am not you, I am the dark Kimi. I eat greylians for breakfast. Where's my prey?"

"What is your prey?" Kimi asked, hoping this dark Kimi could not detect her thumping heart.

"The General. The one who expects humans to bow to him. The one who will tear worlds apart. Where is he?" Lightning flashed, searing the dark Kimi's eyes with evil menace. Thunder cracked and the walls trembled.

"You mean General Cohn?" Kimi asked. That's when it clicked. Exactly as Babbage had surmised. Because this was Kimi's blip, and it had been shared the first time round with General Cohn, he had left his own fear behind – which just happened to be Kimi – or at least a darker imaginary version, the one that Cohn himself might see in his nightmares. "He's dead," she told the vampish weirdo.

"Dead?" The dark Kimi hissed and bared her fangs.

Kimi nodded. "Yep, dead. Killed him myself. Shot through him the gut with his own weapon."

Dark Kimi deflated with a hefty sigh. "So he won't be coming?"

"Not ever. Sorry."

The rain stopped suddenly, as did the thunder and lightning, and the strip lights went back to how they were. The melon-sized bliss flies returned to the windows and bumped against the frosted glass.

Perry, who had come around and was watching this from the floor with his head in Kimi's lap, laughed. "Amazing," he said. "She looks just like you."

"Her nose is bigger," Kimi said.

Dark Kimi sniffed, turned and went back to her cubicle where the door was slammed and locked.

Kimi helped Perry to his feet. "Well that was easy," she said. "Let's try the next room."

Perry insisted that he be the one to open the door. Kimi stood behind, watching over his shoulder as the door opened, hoping to find her bedroom, or at least her bed. It was dim inside and at first she thought the room was merely a duplicate of the room they were in. This would correspond with Babbage's account of how he repeatedly ran into the same room over and over. However, when they stepped inside she realised that, although it had the same windows, cubicles, broken sinks, dripping taps and flickering strip lights, this room was at least twice the length as the previous one. Once again there was a door at the far end.

"I think that's where we'll find my bed," Kimi said, with a strong sense of foreknowledge.

"Okay," Perry said, "But let's take this nice and easy." He ushered Kimi behind him and took a first step, then another, glancing into the cubicles to his left and right. Water dripped. Outside the bliss flies blissed and bumped at the windows. Perry stopped, held up a hand. "Hear that?"

A squelching sound, like someone eating noisily, was coming from one of the cubicles. "I hear it." Kimi imagined some huge brain-eating troll might emerge.

"Is that what your monster sounds like?" Perry whispered.

"No, nothing like that," Kimi whispered back. She was about to ask Perry what he thought it could be when one of the cubicle doors started to open. The strip lights buzzed and grew brighter and the thing that emerged from the cubicle was tiny and looked like a teabag with little arms and many spindly legs. It had eyes of some sort and a mouth that Kimi could barely make out. Perry was saying something but his voice was shaking. He scrambled backwards, pushed past Kimi with fear bright in his eyes and he leapt for the door but Kimi kicked it shut and barred his way.

"Let me out!" Perry yelled. "Now!"

"No way, Perry. If this is your fear then you simply overcome it."

Perry was shaking his head. "You stupid girl. You don't understand."

Behind Perry, the teabag was advancing, its spindly legs making tiny clicks against the floor.

"Then make me understand," Kimi said, feeling awfully put out at being called stupid.

Perry stole a glance at the advancing teabag which had paused while a cockroach crossed its path. He looked back to Kimi with tears in his eyes then turned and ran and leapt over the teabag and sprinted for the door at the other end of the room but before he could reach it the teabag morphed into a long green snake and struck like a whip, curling itself around Perry's right leg and pulling him to the floor. The snake's jaws parted, baring two curved fangs dripping with venom. With lightning speed the snake struck at Perry's thigh.

Perry screamed.

The snake turned, a sliver of red flesh dangling from its fangs. Blood bloomed on Perry's leg. He clamped his hands to the wound and started to cry.

Kimi considered fleeing through the door behind her. But then she thought of the twister. All Perry had to do was activate it and they'd exit the blip. "The twister, Perry… twist it… now!"

Perry was sobbing.

The snake let go of Perry, morphed back into the little teabag and advanced towards Kimi. The only thing she could think of was to stomp on it when it got close enough. Her feet were quite weighty - what with the spurs bandaged to her legs - so she was certain that a good stomp might put whatever this strange thing was out of action. She kept still, one eye on the teabag, the other on Perry as he pulled himself towards the door and opened it.

Through the door and into a dimly lit room beyond, Kimi's bed sat under a familiar window suffused by moonlight and the shadows of the insistent bliss flies. The feeling of relief was enormous. All they had to do was get past the teabag thing and they'd be out of there and taking the Gribbley Grabbley Monster back with them.

The teabag was almost within stomping range. There was no tingling in Little Hand, no mojo building in her brow, but Kimi focused, readied her leg muscles. Not only would she stomp on it but she would squish it and squash it until there was nothing left of it. But when she was about to raise her right foot, the teabag expanded and grew before her. Now it was the same height as her and she could see it was nothing like a teabag at all.

Its body was flat, white, and seemed to have no definable skeleton beneath its pale skin. Its mouth was huge, set in the top half its body with triangular teeth that interlocked and looked as if they could rip a cow in two with one quick bite. A piece of Perry's overall laced with bits of his bloodied flesh hung from the point of one tooth. Kimi swallowed hard as two small eyes opened on the top of its almost square form. Legs and arms as thin as pins were now clear – this thing had six legs and pincers snapped at the end of its arms. "What the heck is this thing, Perry?"

"Don't let it bite you!" Perry shouted. "It's a signature, a creature of infinity. It can jump higher than a star and run faster than any greylian craft. And if it takes your DNA it can steal your shape and devour you through your dreams."

"No wonder you freaked out," Kimi said, "You need to get over here and poke it in the eye."

The signature's toothy jaw opened. "You stink like a sewer," it said. "And your feet smell like dead rats."

"Oh, and it's rude," Perry added.

The signature started to shrink, folded in on itself then stretched, all the while making hideous squelching sounds. Right before her eyes the creature morphed into Perry. It opened its mouth to smile but it was not Perry's white smile… the bloodied flesh and cloth hung from his teeth.

"Oh blimey," Kimi heard the real Perry say.

"Nice," the new Perry's eyes searched Kimi up and down. "I'll wager you taste better than you smell."

"Get away, Kimi! Don't let it bite you!"

Kimi looked to Perry who was still on the floor, grasping at his damaged thigh, and back to the new Perry. The creature waggled its tongue. "Where shall I start?"

Kimi's mind raced. Then she found some hope. As loud as she could, she yelled: "Kimi! I need you!"

The signature Perry jerked its head at the sound of a lock disengaging from the other room. Dark Kimi marched through the door, strode up to the fake Perry's side, looked Kimi in the eye. "You need me?"

Kimi was about to make a run for it in the hope the two would battle it out, but what the dark Kimi did next kept her glued to the spot. "Ah, you want me to stifle the fear, I see. Well, crap a doppelganger, Kimi, I can do no such thing." She placed a hand on the fake Perry's head and stroked its hair. "Fears are friends, you see."

The fake Perry watched the dark Kimi as she left the room and waited for the cubicle door to slam and the lock to engage before turning back to Kimi. "She's much better looking than you."

"Thanks," Kimi said, her mind racing once more.

A look of bemusement came over the Perry before her. He put a finger to his ear as if he was listening to a director. Then he giggled. Then he tutted. Then he laughed out loud. "Marry you?" he said and Kimi's cheeks caught fire. "Marry?" He laughed some more and returned a finger to his ear, pondering the thoughts of the mind he had morphed into.

In a blinding flash of inspiration, Kimi knew what she had to do. She laughed, got the fake Perry's attention, then tilted her head in the coyest manner she could muster and changed the laughter to giggles. "Shush," she said, "You're embarrassing me."

Perry's double seemed to brighten at this. He moved a little closer. "Yes, my darling," it said. "We can live in a cave with a pool full of fish."

Kimi giggled some more, took a step back to counter the creature's approach. "I'd like a quiet wedding," she said. "Just us and the tulpas."

"And children," the fake Perry moved again. "We must

have lots of children."

"Of course," Kimi said. "Lots of children." She reached out for him, took his cold hands in hers and the very touch made her feel sick.

"And I will eat them," the creature said. Perry's blood glistened on its teeth.

Kimi swallowed. "Kiss me," she said. From the corner of her eye she could see the real Perry getting to his feet.

"I'd love to kiss you," the fake Perry said, "Would it be all right if I took your lips off at the same time?" His tongue came out, licked the blood from his teeth and pulled away the piece of cloth and swallowed it.

Kimi braced herself as the fake Perry's face moved slowly towards hers. His hands still in hers, Kimi was finding his thumbs, and when she did she held them as tight as she could. "You've got lovely skin," she said. "I'd love a complexion like yours."

Fake Perry laughed. That's when, with all her might, Kimi stomped on his foot. When his head went down as he hollered in surprise, Kimi brought fake Perry's thumbs up to meet his eyes. The aim was perfect. He staggered back with his thumbs fully embedded in the sockets.

"Tell it you don't fear it!" Kimi shouted to the real Perry who was now on his feet.

"I don't fear you!" Perry yelled in response.

The creature morphed back to its hideous giant teabag self, sank to the floor, and appeared to be in a huff.

"We did it," Kimi said. "That was easy."

"Good thinking, Kimi," Perry said. He limped over to Kimi, placed a hand on her shoulder.

"But I don't understand," Kimi said. "Why would you keep your fear secret? Don't you realise how important this is?" Perry looked drawn and ill, his brow covered in beads of sweat. She took him to the wall and sat him on the floor. The bloodstain on his leg had grown. She pulled up a leg of her jeans and undid some bandage.

"Why have you got bandages round your leg?" Perry asked.

"Long story," Kimi said, tore the bandage away, dropped to her knees, and strapped it tightly round Perry's wound.

"I could have got the signature to do that for me," Perry said. The signature shuffled across the floor and sat against the wall next to Perry. "He's mine now, to do as I command."

"Well I'm pleased he's yours," Kimi said. "I hope mine is a bit more handsome. Which reminds me why we're here." She stood up. "Stay put and I'll go get my monster, then we can get the heck out of here."

"Wait! There's something you should know. Help me up." Kimi took his hands. They felt cold, damp. She pulled him carefully to his feet where he swayed a little but stayed up. "Thank you. Now I have a surprise for you."

It felt like one of those moments in a film, near the end where the hero saves the girl and suddenly they kiss and sweet music plays. Only this time the girl had saved the boy. Perry was smiling.

Kimi did not see his fist coming. Did not expect it at all. She did hear the two cracks though; one when her nose broke amidst a flurry of twinkling stars, the other when, a fraction of a second later, the tiled floor met the back of her head which stunned her and kept her lying there motionless until her senses returned.

Perry was standing over her. There was blood on the knuckles of his right hand.

"Want more?" he said.

Kimi tried to get up but could not. The signature was behind her, its spindly legs pressing her shoulders to the floor.

"Take her to the corner and don't let her move," Perry said.

Kimi was dragged across the floor, propped up in the corner by a broken sink, and the signature stayed by her side.

Dazed, Kimi tore another strip of bandage from her leg to stem the blood flow from her throbbing nose.

Perry dropped to his knees and turned away from Kimi. She could not tell what he was doing but he started making gagging sounds and the gagging soon turned to retching and coughing and then he moved slightly, enough for her to see that he was being sick again. Vomit splattered the floor, dribbled from his chin. He paused, took a breath. "This time," he said and retched again and made an awful gulping sound. His eyes bulged and something popped from his mouth and hit the floor with a metallic clank. He spat out the last of the vomit and picked up what looked like a silver pen. He sat back against the opposite wall.

"That was disgusting," Kimi said.

"Well, you disgust me," Perry said, wiping vomit from his chin.

"We need to get out of here. I need to get my monster. We need to get home."

"Need, need, need. Very needy, aren't we?" Perry chuckled.

Kimi thought about making a run for the next room. She could see through the door and her bed beyond and some shadow under the bed which must surely be the Gribbley, but how could she run with the giant teabag sitting next to her. Under Perry's command the thing could kill her in a blink. One to one she could probably take Perry down and get the twister from him but there was no way past the signature. And dark Kimi in the other room was no use. She tried summoning her mojo but Little Hand did not tingle and nothing warmed her brow. She thought of Bentley, pictured him coming to her rescue but of course knew that she was completely cut off from the real world. Perhaps she could talk her way out of this.

"You broke my nose."

"So I did," Perry said. "Felt good. Maybe I'll break your legs next." He pulled to his feet, steadied himself.

"You should stay sitting down. You're losing blood."

"Things to do, Kimi. Things to do." He came and stood at Kimi's feet, the silver thing in his hand. "Aren't you curious?"

"You want my autograph?"

Perry laughed. "Only if you write it in your blood. Your blood is precious don't you know. This is no pen, Kimi." He held out a palm, placed the silver thing across it, tapped it with a finger. There was a click and the silver thing opened up and metallic petals unfurled into a wheel. He took the base of it in his other hand and held it like a flower. "Pretty isn't it?"

"Ohhh," the signature said. "I hope that's for me."

"Be a good slave and I might let you have a go," Perry told the signature. "But first I'd like to disable this ugly little balancer some more. Can't have her trying to escape, can we?"

All she had to do was get the twister from Perry's pocket. The second she twisted it they would thump back on Earth into Stella's buffers and the greylian guards and army soldiers would take care of the rest. She could return for the Gribbley by herself.

Perry grabbed her by the jacket, pulled her to her feet. She tried to push him away but his grip was tight. He punched her again, this time in the stomach which sent her doubling over and gasping for breath. She saw his boot coming for her face, blocked it with an arm, but the force of his kick almost removed her shoulder from its socket with a sickening springy jangle. She fell to the floor chest first and the impact knocked the wind out of her.

Gasping and wheezing she was yanked by the hair and

dragged up the room by the signature. "My turn," it said as they reached the door where beyond which sat Kimi's bed, but the bed swished from her view as the signature spun her around. Her scream did little to lessen the pain which felt as if her scalp was tearing free.

"Don't kill her, I need her fresh," she heard Perry say.

Face down on the floor with her hair wrapped round the signature's pincer claws she was lifted, the roots of hair screaming to be free. With her good arm she reached for the signature's side; a fleshy bag of white, gripped it, took some of her weight. But that was useless. The signature nipped her fingers with its free hand, nipped them until they bled and Kimi's grip released and she was slid hard across the floor towards Perry who stopped her advance with the sole of his boot on her head. "Get up!"

Kimi tasted the tang of blood. She spat it on the floor, used her good arm to push herself to her knees, moved to the side away from Perry's reach, leant her back against the wall, and sat, catching her breath.

"Had enough?" Perry said.

Kimi managed one nod.

"Good. Do you know what this is?" He held up the silver instrument.

The twister made a bulge in his pocket. All she had to do was get her hands on it, twist it and she'd be free. There had to be a way.

"It's a greylian autopsy tool." He pressed something and the tool's array of petals spun and made a high-pitched whine like a dentist's drill. "I thought I was going to have to dismantle you myself, but now that I have a slave he can do it for me."

"I'm a female, thank you," the signature said.

"Then I shall call you Gorgeous," Perry said. He clicked the whirring tool to a stop and lobbed it towards the signature who caught it in its pincers.

"That's a fancy name," the signature said, shuffling up the floor and coming to a stop at Kimi's feet. "How many bits do you want her in?"

Perry backed off to the far wall. "Break her back first. I can see she's plotting something. These hero types are all the same. Can't have her spoiling my meal."

"Meal?" Kimi said. "You've gone mad. Just twist the twister, Perry. Please."

Perry laughed. "I estimate, Balancer Nichols, that I will be twisting the twister in three days from now."

"Three days?"

The signature shuffled closer. It clicked the tool into motion then off then on then off, swishing it near Kimi's face. "Got to break your back now, smelly little girl."

"Yes," Perry said. "When we leave you will be invisible. I shall arrive alone in the buffers and the soldiers will be frantic as I scream and cry and sob my pathetic little heart out that you died in the blip at the hands of your own stupid, childish, monster-under-the-bed fear."

"Invisible? How?"

"Haven't you worked it out yet? In here!" Perry patted his stomach. "I'm going to eat you, piece by piece. Your DNA will become part of me and the rewards are high for DNA of the purest Balancer."

"You're sick, Perry. Really sick," she said in a broken voice.

Perry smiled. "Gorgeous, my pretty little signature, break the balancer's back!"

Kimi found some strength from somewhere to scramble away, to kick out at the signature's snapping pincer but the signature was far too strong and quick. She was picked up, held above the signature's head, then thrown against the sink on the opposite wall. The sink shattered against her back, rusty water sprayed out, Kimi slumped to the floor, the pain zipping through her in excruciating pulses.

"Back broken, sir. Can I cut her now?"

Kimi's cheek was flat on the puddled floor. The signature's spindly legs shuffled close to her nose.

"In a minute," Perry said. "I need to decide where to start."

"Her fingers of course," the signature said.

There was blood running into the puddle at the signature's feet; blood from her head which throbbed as much as the rest of her. She could not move or feel her legs.

"Good idea," Perry said. "With no fingers she can hardly be a threat."

The autopsy tool whirred into action.

The signature's feet were going out of focus. She felt her wrist being held and lifted. Her vision blurred, faded to grey, and as she slipped away she thought of death and heard the words of an old friend `*one death today*` and with a graceful slide which took away all the pain in an instant, Kimi became a ghost of herself, parting silently from the broken body that was once hers.

She floated in air that seemed light yet dark, close yet distant; the noise of the whirring tool a mere whisper and the laughter of Perry and the signature nothing but a jumble of sound. She was floating near the ceiling, looking down on her twisted self and the giant teabag monstrosity and Perry, who seemed to be indicating with a thumb and forefinger just how small the pieces should be cut.

Her eyes blinked open. The pain had returned. She was back on the floor. Something was happening at her elbows where the tightly packed quills seemed to shudder and jostle to escape their bonds. And at her heels the spurs, once tightly wrapped, were growing as if they too wanted out. Her body trembled, righted itself upwards into a sitting position and Kimi could only watch as her broken nose split in two with a spurt of blood and both Perry and the signature backed off as the black beak emerged from her face.

Perry was frozen, as was the signature. They barely flinched when Kimi's elbows exploded. Bandages and ragged bits of sweat-top went flying. And from Kimi's heels came two more explosions as a massive pair of crow's feet appeared. She felt no pain, only wonder and relief as her body parted down its middle and fell to the floor and once more from the ceiling she saw her old self in ruins and in her place stood a man made of black feathers, with arms and wings and the head of a giant crow. Perry slipped, fell. The signature held up the whirring tool in defence but the crow-man did not attack. He looked up to the ceiling and reached out a feathered arm.

Kimi reached down, her hand touched his and thrust him upwards and the ceiling shattered around them and the crow-man burst free with Kimi holding on to his feathery mane and the feeling was joy and release and a wonderful sense of freedom as they soared among the stars.

She did not have to hold tight to the crow-man's feathery neck; the hold was light and easy with no chance that she might fall. She had the notion that this must be because she was dead and so nothing else could really harm her, but before she could dwell any further on her death and the people she had left behind, the crow-man veered towards a star far brighter than any other. As they grew nearer, the star twinkled as if calling them into its light and Kimi smiled as the wind took her hair and black feathers fluttered around her.

***

14
Divine Intervention

The flight through the tunnel of light took some time. As she floated along on the feathered beast beneath her, Kimi realised, with a smile, that time was irrelevant in death. She felt no pain, neither in her cruelly beaten and broken body nor in her heart for those she wouldn't see again. The memory of their smiles was enough; the knowledge that even death could not break love and friendship.

As the light around her rippled and waved and the wind blew into her enlightened smile, she shouted and screamed and gasped, wanting no end to this feeling, this freedom to fly among the stars with no weighty burdens.

The wavering light evaporated into clear blue sky. A hot sun warmed Kimi immediately. Crow-man stopped flapping, straightened his wings and glided downwards towards the immense beauty of the turquoise shimmer of water below.

They continued the descent and in the vast ocean a small circle of green became apparent and when they grew nearer the green was surrounded with sand and crow-man glided softly to the sand and came to a stop and Kimi slid from his back when he straightened.

The sand was warm and soft like cotton wool. Crow-man was heading for the greenery. There were no seagulls, Kimi noted as she went to follow. No insects. No birds. Just sunshine and softness. She pushed through the vegetation with ease and felt like a fairy on the way to meet her prince then giggled at the thought of kissing a Bellamy's Aunt. She leapt instead of walked. She smiled the whole time, catching the occasional glimpse of crow-man's feathered back before he slipped beyond another tree. With only the light sounds of her own footfalls and the swish of the white dress she suddenly realised she was wearing, Kimi was startled to a stop when a new sound came to her ears.

Her first thoughts were of a bubbling stream but they were quickly cast aside. The watery noise was the splish and splash of oars and the sound was coming from beyond the next bush. Thinking, for whatever reason, that she needed to show some respect, Kimi smoothed down her dress, straightened her hair a little and then pushed through the greenery and into a small clearing.

The old man with the bushy beard was sitting against a tree. He still wore his cap with the mermaid badge and the jumper with snowflakes and deer on it. In the middle of the clearing was a huge pile of silver fish. They all appeared to be dead. Kimi made to step forward, to go to the man, but a whistling in the air made her look up in time to see a silver fish fall from the sky. It joined the pile with a splat.

"Costly business this," the old man said. "Come, join me."

Kimi did. She sat by his side. Another fish whistled from the sky, bounced once and slid down the pile.

The man sighed and a small fire made with nothing that Kimi could see erupted in flames at the old man's feet; a fire surrounded by a circle of rocks which Kimi had not noticed before.

From the air the old man snatched an arrow on a rope, threw it at the pile of fish and yanked the rope and caught the returning arrow with a fish impaled on its tip.

"You'll join me for supper I hope." He thrust the fish into the fire and it crackled.

When the fish was ready he gave Kimi the arrow to hold and to eat from. "Bite and share, bite and share," he said. Kimi took a small bite and the fish was delicious. She handed the arrow to the old man.

"Am I… dead?" she asked, amazed at how soft and how clear her own voice sounded.

The old man put the fish's head in his mouth and bit it off. He chewed on it, thoughtfully, staring into the fire. He swallowed, passed the arrow back to Kimi. "Best bit, the head. Most prefer not though, and that will always be the way."

"I'd like to try," Kimi said.

The old man smiled, snatched another tethered arrow from the air, held it ready, raised his eyebrows, waited. Then came another whistle and the man released the arrow and the fish was impaled before it hit the pile. He yanked it back, poked the arrow into the flames and they crackled.

"Be my guest." He pulled the bronzed fish from the flames and handed Kimi the arrow. "Doesn't come much fresher than that."

"Thank you." Kimi put the fish's head into her mouth and sliced it off with her teeth.

"What did you get?" the old man asked.

Kimi chewed. The tartness made her jaw squirm. "Gooseberries," she said, smacking her lips.

"My favourite. I'm jealous." He grabbed another arrow from the air, speared two fish, cooked them both at once, and handed one to Kimi.

"Hmm, strawberry," Kimi said, chewing on the head.

The old man bit the head off his fish. "Orange I think, or passion fruit. Not bad at all."

This went on for some time. They speared and cooked

more fish and various fruit flavours revealed themselves, some sour, some mouth-wateringly delicious.

"Do you want to be dead?" the old man asked.

Kimi bit the head of the fish he passed over. Pomegranate flavour. She swallowed quickly. "Not really."

"You sure?"

"Am I dead? It feels like I'm dead. I mean, I don't feel like me, I feel different. Light."

The old man nodded, dropped his arrow into the flames. Kimi did the same and the flames and the circle of rocks vanished.

"You nodded," Kimi said. "Was that a `*yes*` nod?"

"Sometimes…" the old man began, "sometimes things have to happen the way they happen. Sometimes there's no stopping those things. Can you see that, Kimi?"

"I think so."

"But other times, something needs to be done; a path to change, a journey to alter, and when one recognises such a revelation, one has little choice but to step right in and take action. Can you see that also?"

Kimi nodded. Another silver fish whistled from the sky and splatted onto the pile.

"Can be a lonely job this," the old man said. "It's not often I get company. Not often I get to step in."

"This is your job?"

"Enough about me. This is about you, Kimi, about changing your course."

"What course?"

"Tell me, Kimi. What have you learnt of your mojo in your first year as a Balancer?"

"I know that it comes from within, from focusing."

"And what tricks can you perform?"

"Tricks?"

"What you can do – what skills you have."

"Oh. I can do good stunners, shoot flames from my

fingers, erm, I do a cool separation, and I'm getting used to doing twirlies."

The old man sprang to his feet. "Show me. Stunners first."

Kimi stood. "My mojo doesn't work here." The old man took a step forward and flicked her on the brow. Kimi yelped. "That hurt."

"Your mojo is activated. Show me your best stunners."

The warm glow was sitting comfortably in her brow. Little Hand tingled. "Nice," she said. Soon, heavy bunches of silvery stunballs hung from her hands. She flung them to the air and they all landed in the sand before dissipating. Kimi looked proudly to the old man.

He was shaking his head. "Like this," he said and began rubbing his hands together. A golden ball appeared and as he rolled his hands around it the ball grew and soon the old man's hands were a foot apart and the ball was still expanding. When he stopped rolling he was holding a golden ball that was so big Kimi could not see his face.

"Wow," she said.

"Too early for wows," came his voice from behind the ball. Then he dropkicked the thing and launched it to the sky where it went so high it almost vanished before it exploded into a cloud of inky blackness which spread across the sky, blocking out the sun. Rain started to patter onto the fish pile, the sand, the greenery – and Kimi's head. Only it was not rain. The tiny golden droplets were mini stunners. Kimi's legs gave a wobble, as did her neck, and she slumped to the sand in a – stunned – daze. She could not get up because the shower was not stopping. The old man was grinning from beneath a transparent umbrella.

The shower stopped and blue sky returned. Kimi got carefully to her feet.

"You can stop whole armies in their tracks with that little number."

"Good one," Kimi said. The old man no longer had an umbrella.

"Flames next," he said. "Show me good control."

Kimi focused on her left wrist. Mojo came easily, perfect rings of power like amber bangles. She thrust Little Hand to the air. Orange flame erupted, shot skyward, exploded in a firework bloom.

"Not bad." The old man was spinning golden rings, like donuts, one at the tip of each index finger. He took them underarm and swung them forward as if he was playing bowls. The rings turned to flaming wheels and spun across the clearing, increasing in size. They were as tall as Kimi when they hit the greenery, tore into it, scorched a blackened trail through it. From some distance in came an awful ear-splitting screech and the crow-man leapt into view above the trees with his tail feathers smoking.

Kimi gasped, and gasped again when the scorched trees and bushes grew back to their previous lush green state.

"What else was there?" the old man said.

"Erm, separation. I can get quite high." At the old man's nod, Kimi steadied her feet in the sand and the separation began without much thought from her. Her head and upper body was already above the trees and rising. In seconds she was swaying high above the small island below. The old man was clapping. Crow-man was basking in a tree top. The beautiful turquoise sea went on and on for…
"Whoaaaaaaaaaaa," Kimi yelled. She was falling, toppling backwards, and she must have looked like a felled tree because she heard old man shout `Timber`.

The splash was massive, the impact hard and painful, the resultant wave sucked Kimi under and her torso went shooting through the water as the separation shrank at great speed, up onto the shore, dragged across the sand, thrashing through the greenery where she re-joined her waist and legs breathless, coughing, spurting water from her mouth.

"What went wrong?" the old man asked.

Kimi coughed, gagged, spat out more water, placed her hands to the sand and pushed herself to her feet. "I should have asked you to hold onto my legs."

"The Balancer loses her balance." The old man laughed. "Have you studied much on separation science history?"

"None at all," Kimi said.

"The teachers will tell you to rein it in, to be careful; they'll set you minimal goals that are easily achieved, but what they don't teach you is the art of total separation."

"Total?"

"Yes, as in separating one body part from another. Let me show you." The old man held his hands out in front. They shuddered, stretched at the wrist, then came off with a plopping sound and landed in the sand before running on their fingers, leaping onto the fish pile, catching the three fish that had just whistled down and juggling them.

"That's amazing," Kimi said. "Weird but amazing."

"It gets better," the old man said. The hands threw the fish to one side and scampered down the pile, across the sand, ran up the old man's sides, and stopped on his shoulders where, with the slightest of struggles, they pulled off his head and threw it at Kimi.

Kimi screamed but caught it anyway. The old man's head stuck its tongue out and blew a raspberry and sprayed her with spittle. She let go of the head and it thumped into the sand at her feet. His hands leapt from his shoulders, retrieved his head, and soon he was back in one piece.

"I could never do the things you can do," Kimi said.

"Why not?"

"It's just not possible."

"Why isn't it?"

"It's just not."

"That's no reason."

"Well, no balancer can do what you do. Balancers use

mojo – yours is like magic."

"There's a difference?"

"Mojo is manipulation of self," Kimi recalled.

"True, but so is my magic."

"*You* called it magic."

"So did you."

"Maybe mojo should be as good as it gets for a balancer."

"Why so?" The old man looked surprised at this.

"Well, if every balancer went around pulling off his head, burning down forests, and making stunner storms, it wouldn't take long before the whole world went mad."

"Another good point." The old man stepped closer. "However, Kimi, you have to *know* the magic before you can *see* the magic." He smiled, and gave a contented nod.

"*Know* the magic?"

"Yes. If you study, practice, know your craft, learn the finer points, master them until you go past mastery and come to something new and vibrant."

"Which is what?"

"The magic, Kimi – the real magic."

"So I have to study?"

"More than that, Kimi. Study, yes, but learn how to look past normality, how to stare until your eyes hurt, how to take in knowledge and create new boundaries, how to think before you speak or act. Learn all that and the rewards are never-ending."

"So if I have a good think, do my homework and stare a lot I'll be able to pull my head off."

The old man was shaking his head. "I'll make it easy for you." He whipped out a hand and suddenly Kimi was rocketing skywards – only it wasn't all of her – just her head, looping through the air, and now falling towards the old man's waiting hands. Kimi squeezed her eyes shut but the landing was cushioned by her hair. "How does this feel?" the old man stared down at her.

"I – I can still feel my body, but not here, over there – it's really weird, like I'm in two places at once."

"Good. Come and get your head back."

She smiled up at him, concentrated on her headless body which was out of sight somewhere behind, could feel her own feet stumbling across the sand.

"Easy does it," the old man said.

Kimi's body came into view, its hands reached for her head, picked it up, placed it back on her neck and immediately it was fastened back in place as if it had never been parted. "Did that really happen?"

The old man nodded.

"What else can I do?"

"Pick a time, any time from your past."

The first thought that came was of her own birth. "My birth," she said.

"Good call." The old man touched a hand to her shoulder and in a blink they were in a hospital delivery room standing beside a bed. Mum was sweating, grunting, legs in the air, and Dad squeezing her hand.

"One last push!" the midwife said and with a final grunt from Mum, the midwife stood up from between Mum's legs holding the gangly, bloodied, wrinkled form that was baby Kimi – complete with a mop of black hair, way too big nose, and a dangling umbilical cord.

"Oh Jack, she's gorgeous," Mum said, and both Mum and Dad were crying.

The midwife clamped the cord, cut it. The baby screeched and Kimi fainted.

She came round back in the clearing to gentle taps on her cheek.

"Pick another." The old man pulled her to her feet.

Kimi brushed herself down, thought where she could possibly go. What would she really like to see again? "I know.

When I was six I got this really cool scooter for Christmas. Dad had it customised, painted all over with animal skulls."

"Christmas when you were six it is." The old man reached for her shoulder but Kimi jumped back.

"No. A week after that. New Year's Day. I left the scooter outside while I went to the loo. Someone nicked it. I cried for a month. I want to see who nicked it."

"Denied," the old man said.

"Why?"

"So you can take revenge? It was your own fault for leaving it outside. Pick something else."

"Okay then. Christmas morning when I open the scooter. I'd really like to see it again."

"Granted." His hand touched her shoulder.

It was dark in Kimi's bedroom, only the palest light coming from the lamp outside. Six year-old Kimi was fast asleep with her mouth open.

"Go ahead and wake yourself if you want," the old man said. "She won't see you."

"Won't she implode?"

"No, of course she won't implode. Go ahead, give her a shake."

"I remember this." Kimi touched a hand to her younger self's shoulder and gave her a shake. "I woke up thinking someone was in the room." The younger Kimi's eyes opened, startled. She looked straight through Kimi, then glanced around the room before smiling. "That's when I realised it was Christmas morning. I thought Santa might have woken me."

"If only you'd known," the old man chuckled.

Six year-old Kimi got of bed, threw on her dressing gown, and crept from the room.

They followed her downstairs where she plugged in the tree lights. The floor beneath the tree was filled with presents but one big present stood at the front. The obvious shape of a scooter was wrapped in silver paper and had a pink bow on the handlebars and a gift tag in the shape of a snowman hung from it. Young Kimi stood before it, motionless, with her hands clasped to her mouth.

"I counted to one hundred," Kimi said. "Wanted to take it all in."

"So you stared at it?"

"I guess."

"Well that's promising."

"Anytime now," Kimi said after roughly a minute or so had passed.

Young Kimi dropped to her knees. "One hundred!" she said and tore away at the wrapping paper.

"You didn't even read the tag," the old man said.

Kimi barely heard him. Tears were streaming down young Kimi's cheeks; tears of pure joy at seeing the beautiful scooter. There was a creak on the stairs and Mum and Dad were standing there.

"Happy Christmas, darling," Mum said.

"Did Santa get it right?" Dad said, grinning.

"Oh Daddy," young Kimi went running up the stairs to hug them.

The old man touched Kimi's shoulder and they were back in the clearing. Kimi wiped her eyes.

"That was lovely," the old man said.

A thought struck Kimi. This reminded her of that film that's always on at Christmas – Scrooge – where the old miser is taken to his past by a ghost. "Are you a ghost?"

The old man laughed. "Not at all."

"Am I dead?"

The old man sighed. "Picture this, Kimi Jo Nichols. Out there in the big blue beyond you are hanging onto life by a thread. You have a broken back, a fractured leg, a fractured skull, a shoulder which will dislocate itself should you move or be moved. You have five cracked ribs, two black eyes, a broken nose, and a cut on the head which is bleeding badly, not to mention the multiple bruises which will form after your death."

"So I'm not dead?"

"Not yet."

"I have a choice?"

"Yes, Kimi, you have a choice. You can choose to join me and the others in this place, others in whose lives I intervened and who chose to stay behind."

"Where are they?"

"Watching, waiting for your decision."

"What's my other choice?"

"I can send you back, Kimi."

"To die?"

"Not to die. No. You might think you're in quite a precarious position, granted. I mean, with your broken back and your cracked head on top of all your other injuries you don't have long left. And even then that ghastly... that ghastly boy is going to spend three whole days chopping you up and eating you bit by bit until he can escape with you in his stomach and sell the contents to the thimbleriggers."

"I've heard that word before."

"We can't allow to that to happen. We just cannot. Absolutely not."

"I don't really have a choice then, do I?"

"You've made your choice," the old man smiled.

Kimi realised that she had.

"I'm going to give you the means," the old man said.

"The means?"

"The means to save your butt, Kimi. Saving your butt will scupper the boy's plans and change the lives of millions."

"Great," Kimi said, "So what do I do?"

"Three things, so listen carefully. The first thing you must do is realise how fortunate you are. Such intervention as this is extremely rare. Not many take the flight of the demon to visit this place."

"The crow-man is a demon? So this place is…?"

"Not all demons are evil, Kimi. Your inner demon has great courage and strength. He knew this day would come way back when you first noticed the spots on your nose."

"So he was always trying to get out?"

"Call it eagerness. Call it lack of practice. Call it whatever you want as long as you realise just how fortunate you are to be here with this choice in your hands."

"I've made my choice."

"Yes, so you have."

"And I realise how lucky I am."

"All right," the old man said. A fish whistled, splatted, slid down the pile. "Second thing is, and you might be pleased to hear this, is that when your demon returns you to your body all of the main breaks will be repaired. You will feel bruised and battered but will no longer be in a life-threatening state. I'm telling you this for two reasons; the first so that you don't get a shock at how you feel, and the second to give you the confidence to complete the mission."

"And, erm, how can I do that with Hannibal the cannibal and his lovely signature waiting to cut me up and eat me."

"Easy," the old man said. He reached under his hat. "Tried to give you this a while back. But you wouldn't bite."

"Give me what?"

He held his closed hand out. "You have no idea?"

Kimi shook her head. "Nope, I've no idea." She held out a hand beneath his.

"Keep it warm," he said. "Flows better when it's warm." He touched his hand to hers and opened it and something pressed against her palm but he did not remove his hand to reveal what it was. "What are you feeling?" he said.

Kimi's mind whizzed. "Good, I feel good."

"And?"

"Triumph, I feel… triumphant!"

"And?"

"Um, happiness."

"And above all else I detect that you feel something else."

"You do?"

"Yes, listen."

Kimi listened and immediately heard it – her own heartbeat, solid and sound.

"Alive!" The old man smiled, and took his hand away. Sunlight glinted off the small glass bottle that lay in Kimi's palm.

"Bubblegum Pink, my favourite," Kimi said.

"And a lifesaver, too," the old man said.

It took a second for the penny to drop and remind her of the huge bliss flies bumping at the windows. "Wow," she said. "That's wicked."

"There's nothing wicked about it, Kimi. It's all for the good."

"I know, sorry."

"You must act quickly. Tell me you remember those three important things."

"I remember."

"And they are?"

"To realise how lucky I am to be here and to have this opportunity."

The old man nodded. "Yes."

"And to realise that when I go back I will not be badly injured and I must be ready to make a move."

He nodded once more. "And the third thing?"

Kimi thought for a moment, looked to the sky as another fish whistled down, then looked to the old man and thought some more.

"You can't remember?"

"Did you tell you me a number three?"

"No, I did not," the old man said. "You weren't paying attention."

"Yes I was."

"No you were not, otherwise you would have asked what the third thing was."

"So what is the third thing?"

The old man looked glum. "I'm not sure I have a good enough pupil."

"You're just being mean."

"You think?"

"Yes. I'm only twelve, and not every twelve year-old gets fired into the blip, has her back broken and then gets threatened with being chopped up and eaten."

"Not to mention facing her fear," the old man said.

"Yes, that too."

"Now you're just whining."

Kimi sighed. "Please, tell me the third thing."

There was a wet rattle in the sky and at least a dozen fish all came down at once. The old man let out a deep breath. "I hate it when that happens."

"When what happens?"

The old man looked at her. "The third thing, Kimi, the third thing is this… whatever you do, don't get any nail varnish on yourself. Okay?"

"You serious? That was the third thing?"

"Yes."

"I'm not that daft."

Another sigh and two dozen fish fell from the sky and joined the growing pile. "You best be getting gone," the old man stood up. "The journey back will be quicker than the journey here. Ready yourself, plan your moves, focus and get the job done."

"I will," Kimi said, getting to her feet as the crow-man broke through the trees. "Thank you for this." She clutched the small bottle of Bubblegum Pink nail varnish.

"One last thing," the old man said. "The action you are about to take may result in the death of Perry Sunder. How do feel about that?"

"His death?"

"Of course his death."

"But they're only bliss flies."

The old man huffed. "The bliss flies of his nightmares, bigger than melons, and if enough of them pump him full of eggs he could explode, or choke to death, whichever comes first."

"Really?"

"Think about the logic of it, Kimi. You have no control over how many bliss flies will attack. Granted you only require enough to distract him, but without that control the attack could prove fatal."

"But might not?"

"There is chance it might not, yes. But it's a slim chance."

"Isn't there another way?"

"It has to be this way, Kimi."

"But what if I kill him?"

"He is intent on killing you, Kimi."

"Worse than that he wants to eat me. He's sick in the head, evil."

The old man nodded. "So you have no problem killing Perry?"

"The bliss flies would kill him – not me."

"True, but you would be responsible."

Kimi sighed.

"Look at me, Kimi."

Kimi looked into the old man's eyes. They were as blue as the sea.

"The chances are high that Perry Sunder will die as a result of your actions. Can you live with that?"

Kimi remembered how her heart fluttered in her chest when she first met Perry, and how she missed him when they were separated by a year in the safe-houses, but this new Perry was alien to her, a Perry overcome by greed. "I feel…" Kimi began. "I feel sad. But I know that I am doing what has to be done."

"Yes, yes, but could you live with yourself? Killing a fellow balancer is not an everyday occurrence."

"Yes. Because this isn't just for me, this is for the greater good."

"That's very commendable, Kimi." The old man looked pleased. "But before you go and do the dastardly deed, there's one more thing I must show you. Ready for one last trip?"

"Where to?"

"Brace yourself." His hand touched her shoulder.

They were back on Middling, at the dodo farm. It was noisy, smelly, and the wind was blustery. Perry, with his back to them, was on his knees, apparently fixing a fence.

Kimi was about to ask why they were here when movement from behind some nearby food sacks caught her eye. Out stepped a little girl in a white dress. She had the biggest forehead and her eyes were too far apart.

"Moonface!"

"Shush and watch," the old man said.

Moonface, on tiptoe, picked up a hefty shovel.

"No!"

"Shush!"

Three more steps and Moonface was behind Perry, raising the shovel.

"Perryyyyyyyyyyyyyyyyyyyyy!" Kimi sprang forward, dived just as Moonface brought the shovel down on Perry's head. It struck with a sickly wet thudding sound. He collapsed in a heap without a sound at the same time as Kimi went through Moonface's body and hit the ground. She could only watch as Moonface picked up Perry's feet and dragged him to the nearby hut marked `pen 1`.

"The bitch," Kimi said as the old man touched her shoulder.

They were back in the clearing.

"What the heck happened there? Was that real?"

"Give me your necklace," the old man reached out, took hold of the crow hanging round her neck and snatched it from her, breaking the chain in the process. He took hold of the small metal crow and snapped it in half. Into her hand he tipped a tiny black device. "You were bugged. The crow that stole your necklace did so under instruction. When the same crow delivered the necklace to your windowsill the bug had been placed inside. The Perry threatening to eat you is an imposter. Now how do you feel?"

"I'm going to kill him."

The old man tipped his cap as crow-man lifted Kimi onto his back. "Plan!" he said with a finger to the air and Kimi felt herself flying high and fast until the turquoise water was a small circle. The stars flashed by and with the sensation of being ferociously sucked down a plughole Kimi went thudding into her old bones and stood before a frozen Perry and a frozen signature who were blinking back to wakefulness.

She kicked the cubicle door in at the same time as she unscrewed the top from the nail varnish.

She tore the toilet seat from its hinges and lassoed the signature with it, and at the same time she swiped Perry's feet from beneath him. He fell hard onto his back.

She kicked the silver autopsy tool from the signature's hand and pulled the toilet seat down over its body.

She pushed the signature over as she splashed the nail varnish in a criss-cross on Perry's shocked face. She did not waste nail varnish on the signature because she knew, just like dark Kimi, that Perry's – or the imposter Perry's – fear, would no longer be a threat once he was taken care of. That was her plan. As Perry screamed something about his stinging eyes, Kimi kept him down with a foot on his chest and shook the remaining contents from the bottle which fell into his open mouth and made him splutter.

His face and clothes were changing. He was now a man in a Hawaiian shirt with a camera around his neck. Changing again, his clothing morphed into the dolphin-like skin of a greylian, and shrank to a smaller form which changed again into white material and blonde ringlets that shook and raged as Moonface scrambled to her feet.

"You bitch," Moonface said and lashed out with a fist which Kimi seized. She twisted Moonface's arm sharply and thought she heard a crack. Moonface squealed and staggered backwards before quickly regaining her balance. She made a dash for the autopsy tool that had rolled and stopped against the wall but Kimi grabbed the passing ringlets and punched Moonface on the nose. She fell onto her backside, rage boiling in her pink painted eyes. "You'll pay for this," she said, pink spittle dribbling down her chin.

"I only wish I had another bottle," Kimi said.

Moonface struggled to get to her feet while wiping nail varnish from her eyes. "I'm going to torture you before I eat you."

"Like I'd give you a chance." Kimi hurled the empty bottle at the frosted window at the same time as she started to run.

The window broke with clangs and tinkles and eager bliss flies tumbled inside.

She heard Moonface's first scream when she reached the door to the third room. She hurried to her bed, adrenaline masking the pains of her cuts and bruises. She tipped the bed over, and there was the Gribbley Grabbley Monster, a ball of leather-gloved hands. It squirmed its many fingers at her.

It appeared to have no eyes to poke and Kimi remembered to be firm instead. "You're coming with me." She reached in to the squabble of hands, turned on her heel and marched from the room, dragging the quivering monster behind her.

The signature, still with the toilet seat squashed round

its middle and looking quite defeated, was staring at the bubbling mass of bliss flies clamouring over Moonface, who was kicking and screaming and trying to pull them from her face. Her scream turned into a muffled choke and Kimi caught a glimpse of a slimy bliss fly probe as it slid into her mouth.

"Now's your time to shine," Kimi said to the lump of leather-clad hands at her feet. "Go and get me that twister."

The Gribbley pounced, burrowed among the plump white flies, batted three or four out of its way and returned with Big Sue's oven-timer. Kimi peeled the twister from its grip and, deciding, despite Stella's buffers awaiting their return, that it would be better to assume a sitting position before activating the device, she sat crosslegged on the floor.

"You're leaving?"

Kimi spun round. Dark Kimi stood in the doorway. She did not look happy.

"Yes," Kimi said. "I wish I could take you with me."

"You do?"

"Yeah. How funny would it be to pull you out at parties or Halloween."

"I'm not meant to be funny." Tears glinted in her eyes.

"Sorry," Kimi said. "I guess people's fears sometimes seem odd to others." The Gribbley scuttled on its fingers and came to rest by Kimi's side.

"Yes, hilarious," dark Kimi said with a smile.

Kimi returned the smile. Moonface grunted, her thrashing slowed.

"I have to go."

"Can't you hang on for a few minutes?"

"The bliss flies are choking her. She might die."

"Exactly my point." Dark Kimi stepped into the room, her cape swaying dramatically. "She tricked you. I mean, crap a cannibal, Kimi, she was going to eat you."

"So you think I should let her choke to death?"

Dark Kimi put her hands on her hips. "Yes. She deserves it."

Gurgling sounds were coming from beneath the bubble of bliss flies. Kimi gripped the twister.

"Wait!" Dark Kimi said. "Think about it, Kimi. If you let her live, then she lives to kill again."

"She didn't kill me."

"No, but if it wasn't for your quick thinking she would have."

"What quick thinking?"

"Carrying pink nail varnish as bliss fly bait. Pure genius."

"I wasn't... carrying..."

"Actually you made me proud!" Dark Kimi lifted her chin to the air.

"Proud?"

"Of course. I admire your tenacious resolve."

"You didn't see the crow?"

"What crow?"

"The really big one - bigger than a man, with human arms and wings and..."

"Don't know what you're on about, but do keep talking," dark Kimi said.

"You're trying to stall me."

"I wasn't the one waffling about crows, but the girl must die."

A horrible retching sound came from beneath the throbbing bliss flies. The one on Moonface's face was pumping its eggs. Kimi could see them through its translucent milky skin, feeding into her mouth.

"Why must she die?"

"They're nothing but trouble," dark Kimi folded her arms across her chest.

"Who? Who are?"

"Greylians, of course. I smelled the imposter the second

she arrived."

Moonface went quiet. Her legs stopped kicking.

Kimi twisted the twister and was sucked into a crackle of blue and golden light to the echoes of dark Kimi's laughter.

***

She was back on the car seat, sitting cross-legged, and it felt to Kimi as though she was riding a magic carpet, swirling through tunnels of sizzling golds and exotic blues, although the imposter slumped on the seat beside her did spoil the mood somewhat.

With no further time to enjoy the ride, they were thrust into real time with a great whump of air, and suddenly sitting cross-legged proved not such a good idea. Kimi shot from the seat, sank into Stella's green buffer mist and was catapulted back onto the seat with a thud which sent Moonface slithering to the floor.

The crowds cheered. Greylian guards and army soldiers surrounded them, and as the buffers dissipated, Kimi saw Moonface changing. Her form crumpled then stretched and altered to the man in the Hawaiian shirt and then crumpled and stretched again back to the face of Perry.

"Kimi!" A child-sized Bentley pushed through the cordon, morphing into the teen version as he ran towards her and then into the old version when he took her in his arms. "That was amazing to watch," he said. "What's up with Perry?"

A soldier with a red cross armband and carrying a first aid kit ran to Perry's side.

"Be careful!" Kimi said. "That's not the real Perry." She looked to Bentley. "Get out of here, fast as you can and save Perry. He's at the dodo farm, the hut at pen 1 – and he's hurt so hurry!"

"Calm down, Kimi," Bentley said. "Tell me what happened and we'll get chief Rehd to-"

Kimi held up a palm. "Stop! Teen Bentley please."

"What?"

"Do it!"

Bentley shrank to the teen version.

"Scoot!" Kimi said.

Bentley smiled and twirled away.

The fake Perry had been lifted onto a stretcher. As he was carried past, Kimi saw the face crumple once more and stretch into the smooth and pale complexion of Moonface, her eyes wide and staring. Just before she disappeared from sight, obscured by arriving soldiers, Kimi was sure she saw her blink.

Guarded closely by two greylian and two army soldiers, Kimi was escorted to the stage and brought to stand before the judge who was in conversation with the greylian Tunahmee. From behind the stage, Phenate Thrawn rose into the air and floated down to stand behind the judge and the director of proceedings. Her grin was bigger than the Queen's hat. "I can't wait to see this," she said.

Tunahmee patted Her Majesty's hand then stood. The crowd hushed. "Premature Balancer Kimi Jo Nicholsssss, you are required here today to bring evidence to back up your explanation of the missing General Cohn and his starbursssssst. Are you ready to comply?"

There was no sign of the Gribbley. Of course there wouldn't be. If she had succeeded in taming her fear then she would have to summon it like Babbage did his clowns.

"Miss Nicholsssss?"

"Yes, I think I'm ready," Kimi said. Instinctively she turned and saw Babbage in the crowd. He tipped an imaginary hat and winked. Was he tipping his hat or was he telling her how to do it? Tipping an invisible hat could signify lifting the top off an invisible skull. She pictured the black lump of leather-clad hands, imagined it tipping its own imaginary hat and then to great gasps from the crowd the surface of the stone she was standing on began to waver and the black hands emerged, settling in a lump as the stone went solid again.

"I so want one," Phenate said, raising chuckles from the crowd.

Tunahmee stared at the lump of hands. "You were afraid of thisssss?"

Kimi shrugged. "I guess."

Tunahmee retook her seat. "Very well. You may present your evidencccccce!"

Kimi placed a hand on the black lump and connected with some of the wriggling fingers. She closed her eyes and thought: *I don't know if this is the right way, Mr G - which is your new name by the way - but can you hear me?*

The leather squeaked as the fingers squeezed hers. *Good. I need you to find my memory of the time Cohn tried to kill me and show it to the judge. Can you do that?* The fingers squeezed again.

Kimi let go, stepped back. Two black-gloved hands rose up from the middle of the black lump, turned in on themselves and began to dig and tear. There was a screeching sound and the first sight of an emerging white bubble started pushing its way out.

The crowd cheered as the bubble expanded. Phenate was applauding and elevating herself to get a better view. The Queen was putting on her glasses. Tunahmee was mesmerised.

Good boy, Mr G, Kimi thought and the bubble grew to the size of a double bed. *Bigger if you can, Mr G, I want everyone to see this.* The bubble wobbled a little then grew further and further and further. The two dogs at the Queen's feet scampered behind her chair. *Okay Mr G, that'll do.* The bubble, now the size of a small house, stopped growing. *Good job, my lovely handy friend. Show them what you've got!*

The bubble's white surface went into a noisy speckled fizzle before clearing into a rich full colour image. The scene was inside the Starburst, from a viewpoint that showed the back of General Cohn's head. He was in the pilot's chair, readying the controls. Outside the cockpit window, the old Bentley was whisking up a twirly. Big Sue's tea towel was waving goodbye.

Then the ship was in the night sky. Chief Rehd's green flares bloomed like fireworks and the ship sped into action, zooming in on Pommy Wood and the two interweaving twirlies. And there were Stella and Bentley on the roof of the Shed – only a blink before the ship was engulfed in blue lightning flashes – but they were there twirling their little arms off and Kimi could have cried. She had not expected to get emotional but this really was like watching a film. The lightning stopped and the sky was blue and the camera of Kimi's eyes moved to Cohn's side and saw him vomit before the screen at his front showed the CCTV image of her parents on the golf course and Kimi's heart thumped and then almost burst from her chest when someone in the crowd screamed. Cohn had pulled his weapon. The other starburst appeared and the other Cohn could be clearly seen and Kimi had to blink away the tears as the two ships collided and began to disintegrate.

More screams came from the crowd as Cohn's eyes burst into black sludge and the crowd cheered again as Kimi's hand picked up Cohn's weapon and shot a hole through his middle. There were gasps as Cohn's tubular tongue slid from his mouth and wriggled on the floor followed by raptures and whooping as Audrey the crow appeared and swallowed it down as if it was a worm.

The Starburst vanished in a smattering tinkle of debris along with the remains of General Cohn and the camera that was Kimi's viewpoint went tumbling down through the branches of a fir tree.

"Keep it going!" someone shouted from the crowd, a plea that was chorused by many.

Kimi watched the scene unfold as she fell into the sandy bunker. Dad was running, Mum a little bit behind him. The three black cats dashed from the bushes; the camera spun as Kimi rolled, firing off blasts of orange mojo and the crowd shouted `Olé` when the first black cat went up in a puff of smoke and again when the second cat was hit and a third time when the third cat was disposed of. More cheering as Dad arrived and picked Kimi up. And that's when Mr G stopped the playback and the bubble retreated into the lump of black hands. *Thanks, Mr G,* Kimi thought.

The crowds in the ranks of scaffolding, humans and some of the greylians, were on their feet, applauding and cheering. Tunahmee stood, raised a hand and silenced them. She sat back down and began conferring with the Queen.

As Kimi waited, the aches and pains from her escapade began to make themselves felt. She must surely be innocent after Mr G's brilliant show. And as soon as she got home she was going to sink into a hot bubble bath.

Tunahmee stood, coughed. The silence that followed made Kimi feel small.

"Balancer Kimi Jo Nicholsssss. Our decision is unanimoussssss. We find you guilty of one charge." The crowd broke into frenzied chatter. "Silencccccce!" Tunahmee cried.

Kimi's legs were shaking as the Queen got to her feet. "Your success in the blip," she began, "is to be congratulated. Your memory proves without doubt that you should be exonerated of any blame for the demise of the greylian general. You showed great courage in your actions. Saving one's parents is not a thing most youngsters have to face, yet you did it with bravery, courage and determination to right the wrongs of a criminal."

"Does – does that mean I'm not guilty?" Kimi said with a cracked voice.

The Queen gave a single nod. "However, using mojo in Earth space without due care and consideration cannot go unpunished."

Kimi wanted to object but didn't have the nerve.

"I need not remind you that, despite your heroics, you are still a premature balancer."

Kimi felt her cheeks warm.

"Your punishment will be a mission of a laborious nature, and will therefore give you time for reflection – reflection on what you have learned from your escapades. You may now be reunited with your parents."

The crowd erupted. Soldiers gathered at the black triangular craft and a door opened. Dad emerged first, then Mum, both still in the grey business suits she had last seen them in; both of them waving at Kimi on the stage.

Without stopping to think, Kimi raised a finger, and twirled herself from the stage and straight into their waiting arms.

***

15
Humility Served

After visiting Perry - who had been found battered and unconscious at the dodo farm and who was in the process of being healed by Adept Nightingale – Kimi went on to BoZone. Mr Purse had helped her on with her new duck-egg blue Time jacket which fitted perfectly, then offered her the pick of the shop and presented her with a replacement crow necklace. Kimi showed great delight at his latest accessory: black leather gloves in honour of Mr G. Anyone who was anyone simply had to have them.

Now Kimi stood at the Shed door with the old Bentley who was making one of Big Sue's tea-towels into a blindfold and tying it around her head.

"Is this really necessary?"

"Shush your moaning," Bentley said.

"I hate surprises." She heard the creak of the Shed door and Bentley guided her inside where the smell of garlic was overpowering. The floor rumbled beneath Kimi's feet and her stomach lifted with the sensation of descent. As the rumbling slowed to a stop, Bentley's hands rested on her shoulders. She could hear nothing, but smelled the fresh air as Bentley walked her forward. If the Shed's construction remained as before they would now be standing on the bandstand.

"Take three steps," Bentley said.

Floorboards creaked beneath her feet, a slight breeze caught her hair.

"Are you ready for this?" Bentley's hands were still on her shoulders.

Kimi hesitated, tried to remember how the place would look. A huge circle of grass surrounded by a wall of arches. And on the grass had been two tall trees. There was not a sound to be heard. She took a deep breath, let it out. "I guess so," she said.

Bentley lifted the blindfold away. "For you," he said. It was night-time. There was no one here, and the place looked as before. The grass and the arches beyond and the two trees, bare and gnarled stood silhouetted before a moonlit sky. But there was something new, standing tall between the two trees. "Lights!" Bentley said and six or seven floodlights snapped on in the trees and swung their beams onto the new construction between them.

"Whoa," Kimi said. She went down the bandstand steps and got close enough so that she could read the plaque at the base: `*K.J. Nichols, Balancer Extraordinaire*` The statue itself was a bronze depiction of Kimi standing with one foot raised on a mound and she was smiling proudly, a bunch of stunners hanging from one hand and a famoose on the outstretched palm of the other.

Then came the sound of clapping as Stella, Big Sue, Rehd, Ruthie, and Granp emerged from behind the statue, followed by Mum and Dad. And then came Stubbs with Cat and Em perched on her shoulders and Kimi was hugged and squeezed by them all to the sound of more clapping as people and greylians streamed cheering and whooping from the arches.

"This is fantastic, Kimbo," Dad said. He kissed her brow.

"You never fail to make me proud."

"And me," Mum said. She kissed her cheek and squeezed her. "And you did it all without using your mojo."

That was a point, Kimi thought, and Little Hand gave a slight tingle. Above the clapping and cheering Kimi heard the caw-caw of a crow. She looked up in time to see the passing bird squirt a gloop of poop which splattered the statue's head. Call it an automatic reflex if you like, or call it fun, but the stunners came and launched themselves without a thought from Kimi. The crow was hit with volleys of silvery stunballs. It tumbled to the grass, narrowly missing the approaching Blavatsky's head.

"Very good," Blavatsky said, still plump with piggy eyes and wispy hair. Although she was sporting a new blue suit which did not strain at the buttons as the last one had.

Adept Babbage joined Blavatsky along with a smiling Patina. Blavatsky raised a hand and the applause died. Hundreds of people packed the grassy arena and some had even climbed into the trees for a better view. Kimi was pleased it was night-time down here.

"Ladies, gentlemen, greylian friends, aspiring Balancers and fellow-Adepts, I give you our saviour, Kimi Jo Nichols," Blavatsky said.

The applause and cheering started up again and Blavatsky waved them quiet. "To save the lives of countless thousands if not millions," Blavatsky went on, "is a feat that might be expected of an adept, or of a balancer with many years of experience. Yet it was a mere premature who saved the masses, a girl with a pure and brave heart." She paused, allowing the crowd to applaud and cheer some more. "This statue commemorates the greatest event in Heart history. This young balancer shall be remembered by and aspired to by all for generations to come. And now, Adept Babbage, if you would be so kind."

Babbage stepped forward. "Despite never once attending

lessons in the Shed, despite still being four years too young for official balancer status, I am proud to announce that on this occasion the rules have been relaxed and our youngest balancer shall from hereon be known as Kimi Jo Nichols, Balancer Elite and Adept in training."

The crowd cheered and whooped.

Adept? Kimi thought.

Bloody hell, Bentley thought back. He was beaming and his eyes glistened in the moonlight. Behind him, Big Sue sniffled into a tea-towel.

"Furthermore," Babbage went on. "In recognition of their standing as great inventors, creators, and, beyond any doubt, heroes themselves; from this day on be it known that Kimi's parents are awarded Adept status."

The euphoric cheer that went up seemed to lift Kimi from the ground, but then she realised she was performing the stretch from her middle and was soon ten feet off the ground – or at least the top half of her was. Mum was laughing and wiping tears. Dad looked happy as Larry – whoever he was, and his eyes glistened, too. Big Sue was bawling. Chief Rehd saluted and Ruthie jumped on his shoulders and bounced and shrieked. Stella was clapping, as was Bentley who looked like a proud granddad.

Someone shouted for three cheers, and as the crowd erupted and the cheers rang out, Kimi swayed in the air, grinning, and feeling a proud warmth – a feeling she had experienced once before, although on that occasion the feeling had been short-lived. She half-expected the crowds to pause and Babbage to fall from a split in the sky, or even a future version of herself flying back in time to stop another great atrocity, but the sky did not split and no future heroes arrived to spoil the occasion. Kimi soaked up the atmosphere until Blavatsky announced that dinner for invited guests was soon to be served at the Rabbit's Foot.

***

Perry, with a bandaged head, was in a wheelchair but smiled as they talked and tucked into various dodo delights.

"All's well that ends well," Stella winked at Kimi. "And hey, it's lucky I persuaded you to hang onto that nail varnish. Told you it would come in handy."

"Er, yeah, you were right," Kimi said.

"So you don't remember a thing?" Stella said to Perry.

"Not a thing," Perry said. Then to Kimi: "I'm sorry, Kimi. She took me by surprise. I should have been more alert. She hit me from behind and knocked me out."

"Don't worry about it," Kimi said.

"And look at poor Gorgeous," Perry said. He placed a sealed transparent flask on the table. Inside was the shrunken figure of Gorgeous the ghost. She was sitting cross-legged and looked really glum. "Sadmachambasar shoved her in here and we can't figure out how to open it."

"That was Moonface's real name?" Kimi said.

Perry nodded. "Infamous greylian shifter and bounty hunter. She's in the slammer now."

"If I ever see her again I'll…"

"You'll do nothing," Dad's voice. He arrived at their table wearing a grin that Kimi knew meant trouble. "Sorry to rain on your parade," he said, "but judicial protocol insists that your sentence is served."

"What?"

"The judgement," Dad said. "Guilty of using mojo in Earth space without due care and attention."

"Dad, that was a year ago."

"Maybe so but one must pay for one's crimes."

"You're joking?"

No he's not, came Bentley's thoughts. Bentley appeared with a jug of pommy juice. He shrugged.

"Your tulpa will kindly escort you to your first official mission." Dad held out a hand and pulled Kimi to her feet.

"You may twirly, Tulpa Bentley," he said.

"Wait!" Kimi said. She left her seat and pulled Dad and Bentley to one side. "There's something I need you to see."

*

Deciding the workshop would be the safest place to reveal the magical parts of her adventure, Kimi pulled Dad and Bentley into the kitchen and twirled them right over there.

"What is it, Kimi? Is something wrong?" Dad asked.

Bentley looked bemused.

Think before you speak, the old man's words came straight to mind. Kimi tried to look serious, and wondered where to start. "Thing is," she said. "That nail varnish wasn't mine."

"Course it was yours," Bentley said, then grinned when he spotted a last cookie by the coffee machine. He picked it from the plate and took a bite.

Dad wandered off and stood before one of the cluttered corkboards. "We really must have a tidy up," he said.

Kimi sighed. There was only one thing to do. The traffic cones and bits and bobs were still on the central table. She swept everything to the floor. The resulting clatter got their attention.

"Please," she said. "Take a seat."

Which they did.

Kimi closed her eyes and thought for Mr G. When she opened them again, Mr G's dark form was squeezing through the wall. Using its many hands it pushed itself free and landed on the table with a thump. Dad and Bentley were all eyes. She had their attention.

"When I was in the blip, something really amazing happened."

"Yes," Dad said. "You saw bliss flies big as melons, you met your dark self, overcame the deadliest teabag in the universe, tamed your fear, took out a bounty hunter, then saved Perry's life. I'd say that's more than really amazing."

"I'm so proud," Bentley said. "Do we get to see it now? A private screening. Wonderful!"

"I suppose if you must," Dad said, smiling.

Kimi found herself grinning. She moved to the table and patted the black lump of hands that was Mr G. "Something else happened in the blip." She looked at the attentive Dad and Bentley with her best mysterious look. "I met a man – a magic man."

"What magic man?" Bentley said. "Are there any more cookies?" he added.

Kimi had already told them about what had happened in the blip, of the dark Kimi, the signature, of how easy it was to tame Mr G before saving the day with her pink nail varnish, but she hadn't told of the magic man, knowing somehow that this was the stuff of secrets. "A magic man, Bentley. A man who could do *real* magic."

Bentley laughed. Dad held up a hand. "What kind of magic?"

"I'll show you," Kimi said. "Or rather Mr G will." She sat in the available chair between Dad and Bentley. "Do your stuff, Mr G."

The lump of leather-clad hands shuddered. Two black hands rose from its surface, jabbed their fingers into its mass, and tore open a hole. The white bubble emerged with ease, inflated to the size of a small car, and was soon crackling with white noise before clearing to an image of the creepy toilets. As the scene unfolded, Bentley gasped when he saw the dark Kimi, and again when the signature expanded to its full size, and cried out in horror when Perry's fist came and filled up the screen. On Dad's request Kimi paused the playback.

"This is not easy to watch."

Kimi got to her feet, went to the table. "It wasn't easy

being there, but it's over now, and I'm fine, and Perry's fine. There's a few more punches and kicks and stuff, but after that – well – a miracle happened."

"The magic man?" Dad said.

"Yes, please will you watch it?"

Dad nodded. Bentley looked uncomfortable.

Kimi returned to her seat and the action resumed. The toilet cubicles flew around the screen as Kimi was punched, kicked, thrown and pounded. Bentley gagged when Perry puked up the small instrument, but then something really odd happened. Both Dad and Bentley were on their feet and so was the Kimi on screen. She kicked a toilet door in, wrenched a loo seat free, lassoed the signature - pink nail varnish was criss-crossing the imposter Perry's face – then Kimi was running to her blip bedroom, the bed lifted, there was Mr G waggling his gloved fingers, and Kimi's fist grabbing him up, and running back to the squirming imposter covered in giant bliss flies, and a close up of the imposter morphing into Moonface and the probe pumping eggs down her throat, and Mr G scrabbling among the bliss flies, returning with the twister, which Kimi's hands grabbed and twisted. The screen went blank.

"Yee gads," Bentley said. "How on Heart did you do all that?"

Dad was goggle-eyed, staring at the blank bubble, watching it shrink back into Mr G's gaping hole.

After a lengthy silence in which the room seemed supercharged with electricity, a silence in which Kimi was certain she could hear the heartbeats of all three of them, she said "That wasn't what happened."

"It has to be what happened," Dad said. "You can't change the memory."

"Something's missing – the man – I – I was taken away, and…"

"Taken away?" Dad stood, joined her at the table. "Taken

where?"

She told them about the bristles on her elbows and heels, the holes in her nose, about how she left her body and floated on the ceiling and took a ride in the stars with the crow-man who broke free from her body.

"You flew in the stars?" Bentley said.

"And that's where you met the magic man?" Dad asked.

"Yes," Kimi said. "We landed on this island, ate fruit flavoured fish, and he showed me what he could do."

"Which was?" Dad asked.

"He could make it rain stunners, he could burn down trees and make them grow back, and he even showed me how to do complete Separation."

"That's a myth," Bentley said.

"It isn't. He took my head off."

Bentley did not look impressed, and Dad looked worried.

"You were in a bad place, Kimi," Dad said. "Traumatic situations tend to throw the mind out of sync and…"

"I wasn't out of sync, Dad. The old man – *he* gave me the nail varnish."

"It was your nail varnish."

"No Dad, I dumped it in the bin at Area 51."

"Stella put in back in your pocket…she said as much. Remember?"

"No because I dumped it again. Listen, there's something else. The old man, he could time-travel. He asked me to pick any time to go back to and we were there in a blink."

"Where did you go?" Bentley seemed a little interested.

"Remember that scooter you got me when I was six?"

"The one I had custom painted which you left outside to get pinched?" Dad said.

"Sorry, but yes, I went back to that Christmas morning, woke myself up, and watched myself open it all over again."

"Let me get this straight," Bentley said. "The magic man

offered to take you to any time, and you chose a scooter? Of all the great events you could have witnessed – you chose a scooter."

"Well, I did go back to my own birth first but that was gross."

"Look," Dad's hands rested on her shoulders. "What we just witnessed on screen were the actions of one brave, courageous girl in extremely dangerous and harrowing circumstances. I am very proud, Kimi. But what you will come to realise is that turning into a crow, flying among the stars, popping your head off, and time-travelling in a blink are merely the product of a troubled mind."

"Your dad's right," Bentley said. "There are many reports of near death experiences where the person feels they have left their body and they float on the ceiling and watch themselves being brought back to life."

Dad nodded. "They often see a tunnel of light and guiding angels."

"You think I'm nuts."

"It was trauma, Kimi. That's all. Perhaps we should get you to Adept Nightingale for a check-up, and maybe some bed rest for you."

She wondered about telling them of twirling home and meeting the old man in Mousehole cave but thought better of it. "No thanks on the check-up, I want to get straight to work. I'd like a real mission please." She folded her arms and felt, for a moment, like dark Kimi.

"Okay," Dad said. "As I was saying back at The Foot, your punishment is your first real mission. Tulpa Bentley, sir, if you would be so kind."

Bentley was looking smug. Kimi didn't like this.

A finger twirl later and Kimi and Bentley were standing in pen 1 at the dodo farm. The stench of dodo poop made her gag.

"Stinks, I know," Bentley said.

Kimi had an idea what was coming next.

"With Perry being out of action," Bentley began and Kimi's heart sank. "I'm afraid the scoopers have clogged up. So a bit of manual labour is needed."

"Was this your idea?"

Bentley shook his head.

"Who then?"

"Don't know. Orders came from above."

"I have to clean all this poop?"

"Yes, and unclog the scoopers, and fill the feeders before the dodos starve to death."

"Every pen?"

"Every pen."

"But that's so…"

"What?"

Kimi sighed. "Nothing."

"I'll leave you to it then." Bentley whisked up the wind and vanished.

Kimi stared around at the all the poop. Piles of it. And the stink was worse than Dad's feet on a bad day. She wondered if she could somehow summon her mojo to help but couldn't figure how that might work. Then she had a brainwave. She hopped over the fence and onto the grass beyond and tipped an imaginary hat to the ground and the grass wavered as the black lump of Mr G pushed through. After explaining to Mr G exactly what he had to do, the monster cracked all of its leather-clad knuckles and set to work, scooping and shifting the poop far quicker than Kimi ever could have. She lay back on the grass and basked in the sun and thought of the statue and her new status and Mum and Dad's promotions and thanked her lucky stars that Perry's bump on the head had wiped his recent memories.

The sun's warmth made her sleepy and for a while she was lost in the tranquillity, smiling to herself at the outcome of her latest adventure and wondering what other chores Mr

G could handle when the sound of water splashing came to her notice. Through her closed eyelids she sensed a shadow blocking the sun. When she opened her eyes she yelped and sprang to her feet.

"Very innovative," the old man said. "I tip my hat to you," he said and did just that. The silver mermaid glinted in the sunlight.

"Thanks," Kimi said, her heart pounding.

"But also very lazy." He didn't look pleased. "I'm confiscating your monster."

"You are?"

"I am." The old man snapped his fingers and Mr G vanished mid-scoop. "You may have him back once you've finished your chores."

"That's so not fair," Kimi said.

"There's a time, Kimi Nichols, when no matter how much of a hero you might be, no matter how privileged you are, you must remain humble and willing to get on with shovelling the crap. Getting your hands dirty is just as important as saving the universe."

The air around the old man began to swirl and he vanished to be replaced by Stella.

"Hello sister," Stella said. "Bentley told me you're in the poo." She laughed.

Kimi stared at her.

"Ach, you look like you've seen a ghost, sister. You okay?"

Kimi nodded. "Couldn't be better." She hopped back over the fence and picked up a shovel.

THE END

Acknowledgements and Thank Yous

A huge round of applause goes to Blaenavon VC Primary School; Head teacher Deb Woodward for allowing Kimi into her classrooms, and teacher Jen Hughes for achieving the impossible, whipping up great support and not to mention the amazing creativity.

To Julie at JD Lewis Photography for getting down with the kids and providing me with many excellent shots for the website – I thank you and your shiny lens.

To the crazy Hannah Prewett – AKA Phenate Thrawn – for nagging her teacher to take Kimi into the classroom, setting the ball rolling for some stunning projects – thank you, you crazy ray of sunshine.

To all my Beta readers for making Kimi Better... I'm so grateful for your time and excellent suggestions.

To Caitlin and Emily Horler and Alia Slater for helping with reviews of *Kimi's Secret* and for getting *Kimi's Fear* up and running. You are three wonderful stars! Thank you.

Thanks a million and gratitude aplenty to Perry Iles of

ChamberProof Publishing services (chamberproof@yahoo.co.uk) for meticulous proofreading and bringing many inspirational suggestions to the work.

To Jane at JD Smith Design for stretching greylian heads, upturning their cupcake mouths and producing some marvellous work on the cover, website and formatting - I am eternally grateful.

Thanks in abundance to Oliver Martin at ommusic.info and mybooktrailer.com who worked hard to acquiesce with my childish demands and come up with some awesome tunes and imagery for the Kimi soundtracks and trailers.

To Jill Prewett and Libby O'Loghlin at Nuance words: www.nuancewords.org for thrusting Kimi into the spotlight, for organising her life, for giving it their all and for making things happen – a most gracious Heartfelt thank you.

To my family for their endless support, and to my wife Ande for her persistent inspiration, and hot cheese scones – thank you forever.

And finally, thank YOU, reader, for reading!

www.kimissecret.co.uk
www.johnhudspith.co.uk

Crow Poem Competition Winners

Huge thanks to all who entered. After much brooding, we have three deserved winners. First up is the category of `young, talented and aspiring wordsmith` and the prize goes to Menna Chapman. Menna's `*sense of richness*` stole the show...

CROWS

Claws as sharp as razors
Eyes as yellow as gold dust
A caw as loud as nails scraping down a blackboard
An evil cackle as loud as a witch's
Feathers as black as the darkest coal
A beak of black like a shimmering black diamond
A sense of richness in his caw like a call of death
"Caw, Caw, Caw, Caw"
The crow strikes again!

Menna Chapman, Year 6, Blaenavon Heritage school
Well done, Menna.

Next up is winner of the category 'kooky curveball from left field' and that goes to the delightfully mad Paul Askew...

THE CROW

I wanted to be able to walk
up this wall, so I sewed
Velcro to my hands and feet.
A crow came over and bellowed,
'What on Earth do you think you are doing?'

I explained myself.
It called me immature.
I said 'That's not fair, you don't even know me!'
It said 'I've met your sort for sure.
Gallivanting around, making noise,
throwing stones at my kids.'
It started pecking my temples.
'Get off my wall! Get off, you scoundrel!'
I tried to swat it away,
but it just flew round onto my back
and started attacking my spine.
'Get off my wall! Get off! Get off!'
Then it stopped. It was still for some time
before saying 'Oh... Oh nuts.'
in a muffled voice. 'What's up?'
'I've got my beak stuck
in between two of your vertebrae.'

I couldn't pull it out coz
it was in a hard to reach area,
so I had to go to hospital.
The wait to be seen seemed like forever
and I couldn't sit down as

I was scared if I leaned back
the beak might sever my spinal cord.

'I'm thirsty,' it said.
'I'll get you some water.'
'I don't want water, I want coffee.'
'I can't afford coffee. You ought to
Be glad I'm giving you anything
at all!' It mumbled something
I couldn't make out.

Finally we were seen by a doctor
and the next thing I knew,

I woke up lying on my side.
In the bed next to mine I saw the crow.
'Thank God for that,' I thought.

We were both going the same way home,
and so ended up sharing a taxi.
I was surprised when the crow
apologised for what had happened
saying it felt terrible. I ended
up going back to its place
for a drink.

Half an hour later
we were making sweet, sweet love.

Paul Askew – age 30
Ahem, thanks for that, Paul. Makes me smile with every read.

And finally, the winner of the category `crows are canny` goes to the erudite rhymester Celia Kay Andrew…

A Murder of Crows

My people are Corvid – I'm Crow to my friends
but my enemies fear me and loathe me.
'A Crow on the thatch and soon Death lifts the latch'
- is this because black feathers clothe me?
Folklore and legend attack and insult me.
All through the ages my name's rung the knell.
According to myth, I'm a soul-bearing demon
who takes the Departed to heaven or hell.
Look you more closely! I'm sure you'll befriend me
when stories from further afield come to light.
It was I who brought daylight to Inuit darkness,
who guarded the young Dalai Lama at night.
My people are Corvid, the brightest of birds,
not just omens of everything tragic.
My press has been mixed, but to those in the know -
I am beautiful, clever and magic!

Celia Kay Andrew (my age is a State Secret: I could tell you, but then I'd have to kill you)
Thank you, Celia, for helping to Balance the scales.

Blaenavon Heritage Creature Competition

I had great fun working with the pupils of Blaenavon Heritage VC Primary during the creation of *Kimi's Fear*. I challenged the pupils to stretch their imaginations and create a terrible creature; a creature capable of injecting fear into the bravest of the brave. A creature so new and original and a wonder to behold yet terrifying at the same time. A creature so **bold and so icky that nightmares might be the places it hides**. A creature so awful in its intentions that even Kimi might hesitate before taking it on. A creature so **terrible in its awesomeness that it would earn a place in** *Kimi's Fear*. The pupils did not let me down. The imagination at work was highly impressive and trying to pick a winner, proved very difficult. After much deliberation, the WINNER, the Star of the Show, is none other than the terrifying…

"SIGNATURE" created by the wicked Lloyd Richardson. The Signature species is a creature of infinity. It can jump as high as a star and can run as fast as an alien space craft. It strolls along insulting its prey even when it's not worth the effort. It takes a sample of DNA from an unsuspecting creature and mutates into them. Once he has a DNA sample he can turn into it at any time. He can also mutate into all manner of different parts of different Species and morph them together to create a super creature. The Signature devours its prey through their dreams. It sends a copy of itself into their dreams. The prey doesn't actually die but it believes it has and so is vulnerable to attack from the reality. The Signature eats its prey while it is busy dreaming about him and trying to stay alive. It looks weird, like a giant teabag with pincers and sharp teeth.

Well done, Lloyd. Your horrific beast did a great job at terrifying Kimi (and Moonface) and played its part well in *Kimi's Fear*.

Blaenavon Heritage Short Story WINNER

I challenged the pupils to come up with a scary story for Kimi – and make me scared, I said.

Not only did they make me scared, they made me laugh, and made me shocked, in fact downright horrified – not to mention impressed. Did I mention impressed?

The standard was so high I'm afraid I could not pick just a winner. I ended up with one outright winner and two runners up. And so, without further ado,

THE MOST WONDERFUL WINNER IS...

Adventure with Kimi by Lewis Gardener

There lay Kimi handcuffed to the bed looking out into darkness.
  Kimi started to panic she screamed "Rehd!
  "Ruthie!

"Balancer Stubbs!
"Stella!"

And then she screamed at the top of her lungs: "BENTLEYYYYYYYYYY!"

Then a very vague "Twit-a-woo" came to her ears and Kimi whispered: "Em, is that you?" Almost as a reply another "Twit-a-woo" came.

Kimi shook her handcuffs, half-expecting them to open but they did not so she focused her mind on the handcuffs and could feel the pulse of her heart beating "Boom, boom – boom boom…" she looked at her handcuffs and pushed hard and felt as though her head would burst with power and then…

All of a sudden the sound of metal bending and a "Creeeaaak" and then within seconds "snap" her handcuffs burst open and Kimi was free. She was determined to find her friends and get to Heart, to Home, to Bentley.

Kimi tried to find a door but then she remembered she could shift and she stretched and stretched and stretched until the tips of her fingers just touched the cool metal. She found some sort of door knob. Kimi pulled this door knob but stopped suddenly, for she felt a big, round, thick button. She pressed her thumb against this button but nothing happened at first but then her cell rotated and Kimi fell, and without knowing she stopped herself a foot of off the floor. Kimi got to her feet and walked to the door and pulled the door open to find a blinding light and Kimi found herself in a narrow corridor and a door marked prison cell no 1. As Kimi walked into the room she heard hard sobs, moans, groans. She walked closer to the sounds of misery and pain.

Stella screamed, "Back again are you? Come to torture us again? Well, we'll never betray Kimi. Kimi could kick your behind to Heart and ba-"

"Stella it's me, it's Kimi, I managed to break ou-"

Stella boomed: "Moonface! How dare you imitate such

a supreme balancer. I know you're trying to pretend Kimi broke out and is here to rescue us."

"Shut up, Stella. I'm really Kimi."

"Prove it!" Stella said suspiciously.

"Okay, Stella, erm let me think." Kimi tapped her chin. "You wet the bed until you were ten."

"Oi! I told you never to mention that again."

Kimi couldn't help herself as she let out a little chuckle.

"Let's get out of here, Kimi. It freaks me out"

"Let's," replied Kimi.

Kimi and Stella went into the other rooms and found Rehd, Ruthie and Stubbs. Rehd seemed very relieved but no one noticed, they were all super alert and they managed to slip past Moonface's guards and burst into the control room. Kimi tied up the pilots and guards by quickly shifting.

"Nice touch," Stella said, impressed.

"Thanks," Kimi said.

Rehd reset the course but …

"BOOM!" one of the guards shot his gun through a gap in Kimi's arm and it hit the control system.

"We'll have to fly manually," Rehd said.

"Okay, we'll do that then," Stella said reassuringly, but then SMASSSSSSSH!!!

"Agghhhhh," Kimi screamed, but still focused, making sure the pilot or guards did not slip out of her hands.

"No, the right engine's smashed to pieces were gonna crash," Rehd said, terrified…

They crashed in a jungle and Kimi managed to move the scrap metal off of the others and together they ran and ran and ran, sometimes hearing Moonface's guards shooting their guns all over the place. Moonface, Kimi hadn't thought of Moonface, could she be dead or maybe-

"Kimi, c'mon," her thoughts were interrupted by Stella's instructions and Kimi fell to the ground grazing her elbow and her knee.

"Whoopsey!" she said as she stood up dusting herself down and now feeling a bit sick.

"C'mon," Stella said, more angrily now, then they ran into a rumble between a signature and a mortem LATOR.

Kimi instantly took charge, "Everyone try and get hold of Moonface and her guards!!!"

"But, Kimi-"

"Trust me!" While the others held off Moonface's guards, Kimi looked into the signature's deep dark black shiny eyes and simply said, "Stop!" in a calm voice.

The creature looked at Kimi, shook its head – and stopped. This creature was now under Kimi's control. She told it to remain still. Then Kimi focused her mind on the mortem LATOR. It lashed out at Kimi before she could do anything and the powerful punch knocked her to the ground. Kimi told the signature to "Get this heavy four-legged beast away from me."

The signature tackled the heavy beast to the ground. Kimi got up and again focused her mind on the beast and after half-a-minute both of the beasts were under her control. Kimi told the two beasts to at least injure the guards and kill Moonface if possible.

Kimi ran to the others. She stood still and closed her eyes and felt a burning sensation like she had never felt before. She told the others to get cover immediately. Kimi felt Little Hand burn with pain and her eyes, mouth and ears felt the same way, then Kimi screamed an ear-piercing scream, white power came shooting out of her arms, eyes, mouth and ears and Kimi thought her soul was leaving her.

Then she heard Moonface shout, "Nooooooooo!!!"

A white light filled the air, just white, it was all over, the power must have killed Moonface. She was gone for good. No more worries.

By Lewis Gardener.

Lewis, this is such an imaginative and creative piece of writing. I love all your little inventions and especially like the scene where Kimi is erupting with white light…very scary. Yet, despite the horrific story you even managed to inject a little humour…when Kimi mentioned Stella had wet the bed until she was 10, well, you made me laugh out loud. Your outrageous humour is a great gift. Use it well!

***

And our 1st Runner up, with a shocking little tale is…

Kimi's Adventure by Lloyd Richardson

"LA, LA, LA, LA, LA, LA, LA," sang little Susan Johnson as she rode her red tricycle to her most CERTAIN doom. She went into the dark alleyway to her house. She was nearly there when it happened a crow came out of some luxurious bushes and attacked little Susan – or did it? It was running away from something. Then all of a sudden a tall dark man came out.

Three weeks later Susan's story was all over the news. "LITTLE SUSAN JOHNSON GONE MISSING." was the headline.

A red tricycle was left outside a gigantic villa. It was Kimi's villa. A note was attached to the trike and it said, *"FOUR MORE DEATHS AND THEN YOURS."* Kimi was absolutely terrified.

The following night Kimi stared out of Stella's window wondering who wrote it. Then a Big Black Shadow swooped down into a brightly coloured bush. A pair of bright red eyes appeared… was it Moonface?

BANG! BANG! BANG! went Stella's apartment door.

Stella was nowhere to be seen. Kimi was alone, "Hello who is it? Stella is that you?" BANG! BANG! BANG! the door went again. Kimi went over to the door and peered through the keyhole. There was nothing there. But then a very cold hand lay on her shoulder. "AAAAAAAAHHHHHHHH!" Kimi shouted.

"Another nightmare. That's the fifth one this night," said Stella in a big brown rocking chair.

A new headline appeared in the newspaper: "THREE MORE CHILDREN MISSING." Kimi gulped "One more, then me."

"Who?" said Kimi's dad.

Kimi handed over the note with tears in her eyes. "I'm going to die soon," she said.

Suddenly a big bang occurred and a big creature blasted through the ceiling and stared at Kimi and said in a crazed voice, "Time to die, Kimi kitten."

They ran for the basement, went inside and locked the door. Kimi's dad turned on the light and stood in front of the basement door thinking of a plan, when a gigantic claw went through his stomach and his intestines were hanging off of the claw and a crazed laugh came from the murderer.

The light flickered three times and then Moonface appeared and teleported to her space ship. "You're finally mine Kimi," said Moonface.

They were flying into the Crouton nebular but it sounded like the engine was falling apart – it was that `thing monster` if you will. It was taking the wires out of the ship. It went to the window and said "I am signature and I want my revenge," and then it screamed and the ship went down like a duck being shot.

Kimi swung her hand round but signature caught it and lifted Kimi. Kimi kicked signature in the stomach and threw some stunballs and trapped him. She asked it "Why did you kill my friends and family?"

He remained silent for a while, then he said "Your father, how much do you know about him?"

"What you mean, before you killed him?" Kimi said angrily.

"Yes."

"Enough," said Kimi.

"So you know how I was made?"

"No, why would I know that?"

"Because Kimi my dear it was your father who created me."

"NO, NO, NO YOU'RE LYING – NO!" Kimi shouted.

"Oh yes, my darling, he created an abomination."

Kimi felt like she had been betrayed by her father.

"Your father created me, but after he did he wanted to destroy me so I ran away and now I want my revenge."

"So it's my father's fault you kill but you need a friend don't you? I'll be your friend." Kimi got up turned round and faced the monster. The signature leaned forward and stuck his long claw through Kimi's chest. Kimi fell to the ground - dead.

The signature laughed and said "Na I'd rather have revenge…"

By Lloyd Richardson.

Oh, Lloyd. YOU KILLED KIMI! Just when I thought you had done something quite beautiful in getting Kimi to befriend the creature, even though it killed her dad, you went and done something quite outrageous, and killed *her* instead. Now THAT is GREAT WRITING!

Furthermore, not only did the actions of your wicked antagonist shock me, but his dialogue, too; so condescending and evil at the same time. Well done, Lloyd. May your imagination take you far and wide.

***

And finally... Menna Chapman. Menna is a prolific wordsmith. 500 words or thereabouts – that's what I asked for, but did Menna manage that? Nope. Menna sent me almost 3000, and a great deal of those words were quite beautifully written and I really wanted to acknowledge such talent. So, even though she broke the rules, Menna wins a runner up prize.

Kimi's Adventure by Menna Chapman

Kimi peered out of a grimy window. Through the dark she saw a streak of dim, white light glistening in the far distance. She peered closer wiping the round window with her jacket sleeve as she squinted to get a better look. Her face was pressed up against the glass. There was another thin streak of light flickering softly ahead like a candle in the wind. Kimi's mind was ecstatic with thoughts swimming in her brain. It turned dark once again. Kimi's breath steamed up the glass. She kept her gaze on the far distance ahead of her.

Suddenly there was a bright, blinding flash. Kimi turned her head, tears welling up in her eyes. The light stayed there for longer than the other flickers, they only lasted a few seconds or so but this one didn't. The light soon disappeared in the same way like the others, first it was there then it wasn't. Kimi couldn't help herself from staring out of the window, her eyes fixed on the dark space. She whispered to herself, "Where am I?" She wiped another tear from her eye.

"Don't worry, I don't know either," said a cheerful voice that Kimi recognised immediately.

"Stella!" Kimi said. She ran over to Stella to give her a hug.

"What were you looking at? I was trying to get your attention but you were in some sort of trance," Stella said looking out of the grubby window herself. The blinding flash appeared again suddenly. Kimi and Stella's eyes watered.

"Kimi," Stella said with an excited face.

"Yeah?" Kimi replied wiping the tears from her eyes.

"I think we're in space!"

"You really think so?" asked Kimi, a shimmer of light twinkling in her eye.

"Well yes, I do think so," said Stella grinning at the thought of being in space. The two girls shared a glinting look for a few moments.

"So, do you want to explore this weird spacecraft or what?" said Stella with pleading eyes.

"Of course I do!" said Kimi smiling a cheeky smile.

"Well come on then, follow me!" said Stella going through a wide door. Kimi followed her.

The tunnel was dark and murky and there was a bright light at the end. Kimi and Stella finally reached the light. They tiptoed inside making sure nobody was there and decided to search in the cupboards. There were three shelves that were filled with glass jars. Kimi noticed a few had eyeballs inside them, the inner colour still bright and twinkling as if they were still in their socket. Others had very large brains in them. Kimi stared for quite a while when Stella suddenly noticed a tube of something with a green colour.

"What do you think it is?" asked Kimi.

"Um, slime," Stella said, looking as if she wanted to be sick. They wandered through a door that had a metal handle. Stella wanted to explore some other rooms on the spacecraft but Kimi started to feel as if they were being watched by someone or something….

"CRASH! BANG! CRASH! BANG!" something was attacking the spaceship! "Hold on to something – quick!" Stella yelled as she jumped for a nearby desk. Kimi slid under the table with Stella holding her hand. They both closed their eyes wishing for the craziness to stop.

Kimi woke up on the cold, hard floor. "Stella?" Kimi said helping herself up. There was no answer. Kimi's eyes welled up with tears. They rolled down her pink cheeks. She looked all around her but there was no escape from the metallic looking room. Kimi was alone, or was she?

"Kimi," said a screeching, sly voice. Kimi spun her head around. Little Hand tingled. Kimi didn't like where this was going but she didn't know what to do. She delved into her pocket and grasped her hand around her mobile phone. Kimi wanted to phone Stella but she quickly realised that she was still in space when a shooting star flew past the window. "Why isn't there any signal in space?" Kimi said loosening her grip on her mobile. "Now what do I do? I haven't got a clue about space! I just want Stella back!"

"TALK! NOW!" yelled Spiker. Stella was fastened to a titanium wall, her arms blocked by titanium bands to stop her from running. Her feet were fastened to the floor, stuck there by green slimy goo that looked familiar.

"NO! NOW LET ME GO YOU UGLY THING!! I DON'T CARE WHAT YOU ARE OR WHO YOU ARE JUST LET ME GO!!" shouted Stella at the top of her lungs.

"I know you know a little girl that goes by the name of Kimi," said Spiker slyly. He looked at Stella with an evil grin. Stella remained silent.

Spiker continued, "I need you to bring her here for me to have a little chat with her. Do you understand?" he said, sitting down in a huge, grey chair.

"I'm not doing ANYTHING for YOU!" Stella said trying to pull her feet out of the goo.

"Oh, but dear Stella, you haven't got much of a choice!" Spiker said cackling with evil laughter. Stella closed her eyes and thought of Kimi. She wanted to protect her not capture her.

"What will you do to me if I don't get Kimi?" Stella said, feeling braver.

"This!" Spiker said. Three of Spiker's guards appeared through laser transport. They each had a gooey stick and started to stretch it.

"You will be stretched," Spiker said cruelly. He laughed again, it was an evil laugh. Stella had a decision to make. A very difficult decision.

"Kimi!" it was that voice again. Kimi didn't like it. She heard it again. "Kimi!" it was in a whisper this time. Kimi covered her ears so she couldn't hear it but she still could, in her mind. Kimi shook her head to try to shake out the dreaded voice. Kimi shut her eyes tight wishing and wishing for the torture to stop. She hadn't wished so hard in her life. "Kimi!" it was back again, like a spinning fairground ride going round and round in her head. Her eyes were still shut tight. She thought of Stella, thought so hard she pictured she was in the room with her. Kimi opened her eyes. They needed time to adjust to the light. Kimi noticed a dark hooded figure standing by an old desk. Kimi rubbed her eyes. When she looked again the figure was gone. She was still alone. Kimi wanted Stella. Kimi always wanted Stella. Stella was Kimi's treasure. She never left Kimi behind and Kimi never left Stella behind.

Meanwhile the evil genius Spiker still had Stella trapped in his secret laboratory. Stella's eyes skimmed the shelves of glass jars. Stella's facial expressions changed from curiosity to horror. Spiker set out his lab table with test tubes and weird ingredients laid out on a snow white sheet. There was a giant, black cauldron. Spiker put on a clean white lab coat. He started pouring coloured liquids into the cauldron then he added disgusting slimy things.

"Aha it is complete at last!" said Spiker smiling the evilest smile. Stella turned her head away from Spiker to try to ignore him. She didn't want to be part of an evil plan.

"Try this now!" Spiker said slowly walking towards the stuck Stella. She shut her mouth tight sealing her lips together. "Open up and drink!" Spiker said moving to tip the liquid into her closed mouth. "Come on drink up, it tastes delicious!" said Spiker using his sweet voice. Then he cackled with laughter. Stella refused to take the potion. She didn't know what it was and she didn't want to find out. "DRINK IT!" shouted Spiker in a terrifying voice. Stella opened her mouth a little bit then without any time to stop him Spiker poured the liquid in.

"That's gross!" Stella shouted.

"What did you expect Stella? It is an evil potion for an evil plan!" Spiker said cruelly. Suddenly Stella's face turned from bright to blank. Her expression was wiped out. Her face was as white as paper.

"It worked!" Spiker said with a flash of delight glowing on his face. He threw the empty potion glass over his shoulder. It landed with a loud smash! "Now, you will go and get Kimi!" Spiker said in a controlling voice. "Stand here!" he demanded. Stella stood on a white cross. A blinding laser beamed down to take Stella to Kimi. When Stella disappeared Spiker laughed an evil cackle. "Haaa, Haaa, Haaa!"

Kimi sat there alone. She had never felt more scared. Her stomach rumbled with starvation. Kimi tried to get to sleep but her stomach continued to rumble and rumble and rumble. She was so hungry that she started imagining things. She saw a figure that looked familiar. She rubbed her eyes.

"Stella! Where were you? What happened?" Stella didn't answer. Kimi's face turned with worry. "Stella! What's wrong?!" Kimi said her throat very dry. There was still no answer. Stella grabbed Kimi's arm and pressed a button on her watch. The laser beam appeared again. Kimi covered her eyes with her arm to block the blinding flash.

Kimi felt herself being transported from the bright ship to the dark lab. Stella led Kimi to a darkened room. Stella left. Kimi was alone again.

"Hello, Kimi!" She turned around to see a large, dark figure. It was Spiker.

"Who are you?" said Kimi with curiosity.

"Oh so sorry, I forgot we never met. I am evil genius Spiker. You might not know much about me but I know lots about you," Spiker said with an evil grin.

"What have you done with Stella?"

"Don't worry, your friend will be fine. The potion will wear off in a bit. It is you I'm after Kimi," Spiker said taking a few steps towards her.

Kimi stepped back. "Why do you want me?"

"It's because of your brain, Kimi. Your brain!" Spiker said stepping closer still.

"My brain? What would you want with my brain? It's just a normal brain, there's nothing special about it is there?" Kimi said biting her lip.

"Power. I want power Kimi and your brain will help me!" Spiker said smiling and showing his disgusting teeth.

Kimi ran. She ran for her life. Her feet pounded with pain. Spiker was running behind her slipping on the floor as he went. Kimi turned into a corridor. There were doors along both sides. She tried them all. All locked. Kimi sprinted towards an open window but she suddenly remembered. "Stella! I forgot her!" Kimi turned around and ran the other way. She saw Spiker running straight at her holding out his arms to grab her. Kimi slid under his legs. She jumped back up onto her feet and kicked Spiker hard in the backs of his shins. He fell to the ground howling and Kimi ran away back to the lab.

Stella was sitting in a corner crying. "Stella?"

"Kimi!" Stella said running across the room to give Kimi a big hug. They stayed there for a while enjoying the company of each other. Then they ran. They ran for their lives. All of a sudden the evil Spiker crossed their path.

"Ahhh you thought you could get away? Well you were

wrong!" Spiker said closing in. The two girls didn't know what to do. Kimi mouthed something to Stella that Spiker didn't understand. Stella's foot twitched ready to run to safety. Kimi winked at Stella. She understood what Kimi meant. Stella ran away down the opposite corridor. Kimi stayed there staring into Spiker's poisonous looking eyes. Kimi raised her foot quickly and lunged it into Spiker's ugly face. Spiker fell back shocked at what Kimi had just done. She hoisted herself up into a trapdoor in the ceiling. Spiker looked up and tried to grab Kimi's trailing foot but Spiker tripped over Kimi's stranded shoe. Kimi was in the venting system. Spiker could hear her crawling through the long, metal tubes. Kimi stopped. Spiker was following underneath. Spiker listened hard standing underneath a vent opening. Kimi removed the little door and leapt onto Spiker's back. He fell to the ground. Kimi grabbed a sharp piece of loose metal and turned Spiker's face around and stabbed it into his eye. Blue blood dripped down his face. Spiker screamed a painful scream. Kimi was terrified but continued killing Spiker. She lunged the weapon into his chest. Spiker started to wheeze uneasily.

Stella ran up the corridor noticing Spiker on the floor and slowing down to look at the horrifying sight. Stella couldn't say anything. Kimi looked up, Spiker's blood dripping off the piece of metal and onto her clothes.

"Kimi, I think we'd better go," Stella said pulling Kimi up from the damp floor covered in Spiker's blood. Kimi looked down on the dead body of Spiker and turned to walk away.

By Menna Chapman.

Menna, congratulations. You have enormous talent in that you know how to manipulate your word choice to get the best effect (scary in this case) for reader. You create a wonderful sense of gloom right from the off with that distant light like a candle on the wind. And there's some lovely gruesome detail like those eyes in the jars, twinkling as if they are still in their sockets. It is these images which give flesh to your story, these images which form themselves in reader's mind and stay with them for hours and sometimes days, these images which remind reader of what a great writer you are, these images which prod reader into reading your other work. Keep it up, Menna. I've a feeling that words will be your living. Come and look me up when you're Prime Minister.

***

Massive thanks and congratulations to Lewis, Lloyd and Menna. Writers for the future!

www.kimissecret.co.uk
www.johnhudspith.co.uk

Lightning Source UK Ltd.
Milton Keynes UK
UKOW040845141212

203639UK00001B/1/P

9 781781 769843